# BLOOD AND GROOM

# BLOOD AND GROOM

# Jill Edmondson

A Sasha Jackson Mystery

DUNDURN PRESS
TORONTO

Editor: Michael Carroll
Design: Courtney Horner
Printer: Webcom

Library and Archives Canada Cataloguing in Publication

Edmondson, Jill
      Blood and groom / by Jill Edmondson.

(A Sasha Jackson Mystery)
(A Castle Street mystery)
ISBN 978-1-55488-430-8

      I. Title.  II. Series: Edmondson, Jill.  Sasha Jackson
Mystery.  III. Series: Castle Street mystery

PS8609.D67B56 2009      C813'.6      C2009-903254-6

1  2  3  4  5    13  12  11  10  09

  Conseil des Arts du Canada    Canada Council for the Arts    ONTARIO ARTS COUNCIL CONSEIL DES ARTS DE L'ONTARIO

We acknowledge the support of The Canada Council for the Arts and the Ontario Arts Council for our publishing program. We also acknowledge the financial support of the Government of Canada through the Book Publishing Industry Development Program and The Association for the Export of Canadian Books, and the Government of Ontario through the Ontario Book Publishers Tax Credit program, and the Ontario Media Development Corporation.

Care has been taken to trace the ownership of copyright material used in this book. The author and the publisher welcome any information enabling them to rectify any references or credits in subsequent editions.

*J. Kirk Howard, President*

Printed and bound in Canada
www.dundurn.com

| Dundurn Press | Gazelle Book Services Limited | Dundurn Press |
|---|---|---|
| 3 Church Street, Suite 500 | White Cross Mills | 2250 Military Road |
| Toronto, Ontario, Canada | High Town, Lancaster, England | Tonawanda, NY |
| M5E 1M2 | LA1 4XS | U.S.A. 14150 |

*To D. with love. I know you do.*

# acknowledgements

Warm fuzzy thanks to a wonderful group of lifelong friends, especially Jennifer Young, Adam Childs, Jackie Chapman, and Stéphane Quinty. Thanks for listening and being supportive, and getting me through all the meltdowns. A special thank-you also to Derek for getting me through the darkest days and making me smile again.

# Tuesday, April 7, 11:30 a.m.

Some women seemed naked without makeup. Other women seemed naked without jewellery. The uptight Manolo-shod Chihuahua who had barged into my office without an appointment seemed naked without an entourage. I put down the current issue of *Billboard* and listened.

"I thought that bullshit about till death do you part only applied to couples who actually got married. That bastard Gordon dumped me and got himself killed four months later. I didn't do it, but I'd like to thank whoever did."

Listening to the little bottle-blond bitch barking at me, I automatically figured the guy who had dumped her must have had a good reason. "So, Christine, what would you like me to do for you?"

She looked down her nose at me. "Isn't it obvious, Sasha?"

*Hmm ... isn't it obvious you're a shrew in Chanel?*

She got up from the faux leather chair opposite my desk and brushed the back of her skirt as if the imitation rawhide had left authentic cowpies on her designer suit. "Everyone thinks I killed Gordon, and believe me, I wanted to. Everyone except the police, that is. They questioned me. They interviewed my family and my friends. They checked my alibi and went to all the places I said I'd been. They found nothing because there was nothing to find, so I was never charged."

She continued to pace around my minimalist-by-accident, barren-by-bank-account office, her ring-less left hand anxiously twirling her hair. I silently smirked that my own blond hair would never have the mousy brown roots hers did.

"So why bother?" I asked. "You should just move on and forget about him."

"Well, Sasha ..." She drew out my name in the same tone people used on a two-year-old who had just discovered the treasures hidden deep inside his nostrils. "I bother because people still talk, they point and whisper, I know they think I did it, and they think I got away with it. When I go to fundraisers or events, they treat me differently. When I'm at the club, they make me feel funny. Trust me, if I'd killed the bastard, I'd be bragging about it."

"So being accused of murder is shameful, but actually doing it is fine?"

"Exactly. If I'm going to get credit for something, I'd prefer it be for something I really did do."

"Of course. But why now? He was killed eight months ago."

"Nine months."

"Whatever. A while ago."

"I was at Monsoon for a dinner date last night. Gordon's cousin Rebecca saw me there. She never liked me, and my date and I happened to be seated at a table right across from Rebecca and her friends. When she saw me, she walked over to my table, called me a bunch of names, said I got away with murder, and then she threw her drink in my face."

"Ouch."

"On top of that, my date, a really hot proctologist named Randall, made up some bullshit about a reminder on his BlackBerry and bailed on our night out."

"That sucks. So ... why me then? I don't really do this kind of work. I mostly do background checks for corporate hires and the occasional cheating partner. I've never investigated a murder."

"Because you're all I can afford."

"Gee, you know someone with an ounce of graciousness would have answered that differently."

"Don't be so touchy. I didn't mean it that way."

I stared at her silently.

"Okay. Sorry."

It was true my rates were low, at least for now. I'd graduated from Sheridan College's Security and Investigator Diploma Program a few months ago and was still trying to build my reputation and my client base.

"I'll see what I can do, but I can't make any promises, and I won't commit beyond one week. I don't see the point of wasting my time or your money."

"I'll be expecting results much sooner than that," Christine said. "And daily reports."

I pointed out to the sabre-toothed socialite that expenses weren't included in the bargain prices of my stellar but novice services. She took a chequebook out of her Ferragamo purse and filled in the details using a ninety-nine-cent disposable pen with blotchy ink. Her signature, Christine Arvisais, was loopy and flowing, and she topped all the *i*'s with little circles. That seemed so very cutesy and incongruous with what I'd seen of her personality.

"So the police must have checked out your story," I said.

"Of course, they did, and it's not a story. It's the truth. My mother and I go to the Crystal Cove spa on the first weekend of every month. We go early Saturday morning, get the seaweed wrap, chemical peel, and mud bath, and then we have a facial and mani-pedicure."

"Sounds like perfect mother-daughter bonding." Not something that appealed to me, since my mother had been out of my life since I was two. And not a way I'd choose to spend a weekend. Too expensive and too chi-chi for me.

"Then a Shiatsu massage and Bikram yoga in the afternoon."

"I'm sure it's lovely." I could never see the point of yoga as a part of a fitness regime — too passive, and too easy to slip into a coma and call it a workout.

"The spa does a weekend cleansing and detoxification, so we get there at eight on Saturday morning and leave Sunday afternoon. We drink twelve litres of water, plus some restorative beverages and a couple of herbal teas. You should try it."

"Only if they spike the tea with vodka."

She raised an eyebrow at me. "We leave refreshed, and about two or three pounds lighter, though you obviously don't need to worry about your weight. Anyhow, they know me and they'll tell you I was there that weekend like usual."

"Of course. Mud baths are important."

"Exactly. So that's my alibi."

"Well, then if you didn't kill him, who do you think did?"

"I have no idea, and I don't care, except maybe to thank them, and to bitch them out for making it look like I did it. Mostly to thank them, though."

"Like I said, if not you, then who?"

She examined her cuticles and seemed to silently condemn the manicurist who had performed her latest claw sharpening. "There were people who didn't like him, and people who did, like with most people." Eloquence was clearly not her forte. "I can't think of anyone who would've wanted him dead, though, except me. He dumped me, completely embarrassed me, and made a fool of me four months before our wedding. I'd already been fitted for the dress — a Vera Wang, with a sweetheart neckline, made of hand-beaded pure silk."

"You can use it next time." Something told me that Christine would probably have enough husbands throughout her life to start her own baseball team.

"Good God, no. It's cursed now, so I put it in a consignment store to recover some of the cost, but it still hasn't sold."

"It's just waiting for the right bride-to-be."

"The invitations had just come from the print shop two days before Gordon lost his mind and turned into an asshole. I was about to mail them out, but still hadn't decided whether or not to invite Mindy Melnyk, who used to be my best friend in high school, but —"

"Can you fast-forward? I don't really care about Mindy." Boy, did that interruption net me a dirty look.

"Anyway, Sasha, after he dumped me, I never really spoke to him again. I had nothing more to do with him or his family and I steered clear of his friends, so I don't know what could've happened to him in that time to make someone want to kill him." Christine was now briskly pacing my office as she spoke. The rhythm of her steps echoed the brusque, staccato delivery of her story.

"Do you think the reason he dumped you had anything to do with the reason he was killed?" I asked.

"I don't know. He never gave me any real explanation, except that he wasn't ready."

I could think of any number of reasons why Gordon might have dumped Christine, and most of them also pointed to motives for him to have killed her, not vice versa.

"I'll want to talk to the people who were close to him. Where does the drink thrower —"

"Rebecca."

"Right. Where does Cousin Rebecca work?"

Anyone bearing such strong animosity toward Christine would be interesting to talk to.

"At Chadwick's in Yorkville. She thinks she's hot shit, but really, she's nothing more than a sales girl."

My office was only a short walk north to Yorkville, Toronto's toniest shopping mecca, which was the polar opposite of the sleazy area south of Bloor, off Yonge, where my office was located. Instead of having a view of the Beautiful People walking past marble-fronted centres of conspicuous consumption, my office window overlooked a dollar store, a body piercing shop, a tattoo parlour, and a Money Mart.

"I guess I'll get right on this and go talk to her."

I figured there was no time like the present to find out what investigating a murder was supposed to feel like.

# Tuesday, 1:10 p.m.

If there was such a thing as a down-to-earth blueblood, then Rebecca Blackmore was it. Think Noxzema girl meets Dolce and Gabbana. Contrary to the outdoorsy, all-natural glow, she was the cosmetics manager at Chadwick's, an über-snooty fashionista store where I couldn't even afford to window-shop. I felt completely inadequate in my Birkenstocks and jean jacket, but the early spring warmth had inspired me to ditch my full-length mink.

"Rebecca?"

The glass doll looked up from the counter. "Yes, what may I do for you?" Although she was speaking at a normal volume, her voice unrolled in a melodic whisper.

"I'm Sasha Jackson. Can I chat with you for a moment?"

"Certainly. Are you interested in a makeover? I can book you an appointment."

Didn't my cheeks already have a healthy glow? "Actually, this might be best in private. It's about your cousin, Gordon. Do you have a break soon? Maybe we can have a coffee?"

"It's quiet right now. Amanda can keep an eye on things. Let me get my purse and I'll meet you at the coffee shop in the food court."

---

I had grabbed a seat at the quietest table I could find. When Rebecca joined me, she gracefully crossed her legs and sat so perfectly postured she looked like an entrant in a dressage competition.

She spoke very slowly. "Yes, Gordon and I were very close. We're three months apart. What do you want to know about him?" She sniffed and brushed the tip of her nose. I offered to get her some tissue, but she said no thanks.

"My allergies seem to be acting up," she said.

I launched into an impromptu spiel. "I'm a psychology grad student at the University of Toronto. I'm looking at the long-term effects of violent deaths on the mourners."

I had honed my ad-libbing skills during my rocker chick band days. Nothing was more embarrassing than forgetting the lyrics to someone else's top-ten song. There was also nothing less satisfying than playing other people's hits to rooms full of drunk guys who wanted to hit on you because they thought you made eye contact with *them* during that romantic/sexy song at last call. When it came to bullshit, I had the market cornered.

Rebecca took a dainty sip of her latte, and I tried to picture her hurling a drink in Christine's face the night before. It didn't compute. This was a classy chick, and if not exactly congenial, she was certainly cordial. Drink tossing seemed beneath her.

"Well, it's really hard when death is sudden like that."

Her soft voiced cracked a bit, but there was no way this model of privileged decorum would have an emotional meltdown in public. She took another tiny sip and carried on.

"You never expect a murder to happen to someone in your own family." She paused for a moment as if lost in a fuzzy old memory. "It's supposed to be some nameless face in the newspaper. But then suddenly your world explodes and you have this never-ending hole. You feel suspended. You never get to say goodbye."

"I suddenly lost someone, too, and I understand how hard it can be. Maybe that's why this field of study appeals to me. It's a kind of closure in a way."

God strike me down for telling that whopper. I felt uneasy about telling such a creepy lie, and the superstitious side of me felt paranoid now for having tempted fate. I made a mental note to call Dad later today.

Rebecca continued. "I think my mom had given up hope on having a second child. Mind you, she was only thirty-three, but my brother, Darren, was already eight years old, and they wanted to give him a little brother or sister to grow up with." She paused for another sip, and I waited for her to continue.

"By that time, no one expected my Aunt Maureen — she's my mother's older sister — well, no one expected Aunt Maureen to have a child, either." Rebecca sniffed and brushed her nose again. "But then, surprise, both sisters were pregnant at the same time. Aunt Maureen was thirty-nine when she had Gordon, and my mom had me three months later. Gordon and I were inseparable from day one. We were in the same classes from kindergarten right through high school. Darren is so much older than I that I've always felt Gordon was more like my brother than Darren."

Rebecca's cell phone twittered to life. She glanced at the call display. "It's the store. Just give me a moment please." She went off to one side of the food court and then stepped out of view.

Okey-dokey. I had twenty seconds, max. I dug right into her purse. Even though the topic of our discussion was sad, Rebecca had shown no signs of tears. That sniffling and twitchy nose had me and my suspicious nature wondering about drugs. Cocaine was and always had been the preferred recreational escape among people with the money to indulge in it.

Keys, Percocet, condoms, breath mints, sunglasses, OxyContin, tissues, Paxil, Percocet, nail file, lipstick, lip balm, Vicodin, and wallet. I flipped open the wallet. Forty dollars. Some business cards, miscellaneous memberships, and the usual plastic. Well, the mood-altering prescription narcotics certainly explained the stoned Mona Lisa serenity.

Not willing to press my luck any further, I closed the bag, but not before lifting her wallet and sticking it in my pocket. I was the picture of innocence when she returned to our table a moment later.

"Sorry about that. I'll have to go in a minute. One of our distributors is on her way, and she has samples of the new summer colours. Anyway, where were we?"

"Gordon's murder must have been hard to deal with." I had all the finesse of a jackhammer.

"It was twice as hard because Christine got away with it." Nose twitch and sniffle number five.

"Why do you think she was the killer? I understand the police questioned her and checked her alibi. They never charged her."

Rebecca sprinkled a bit of cinnamon on her java, then absently swirled the stir stick in the foamy beverage and watched the powdery grains disappear. "She's slippery. Christine would never pull the trigger, but I believe she pulled the strings. It would be darn hard to convince me of anything else."

"What would her motive be?"

"Revenge, because Gordon broke off their engagement." Another pause. "Thank goodness he did. He was too good for her. I never liked her, and she knows it."

"So you convinced him to end it?"

"Yes. Gordon and I had a heck of a fight about it. I'd also fought with Christine about their relationship. She treated him like dirt. I told her I'd stop the wedding one way or another."

"Then Christine knows he called it off because of you?"

"Absolutely. She mailed me a sample of the invitation a couple of days earlier. I know this was catty, and I shouldn't have done it, but after they broke up, I wrote 'I told you so, now go to hell' on the invitation and mailed it back to her."

"Not to be crass, but that seems more like a motive for her to kill you, not Gordon. What does your brother think?"

"Darren and I haven't really talked about it much. My family's very much the British-stiff-upper-lip kind. We don't discuss emotions or unseemly topics. It just isn't done."

"I see." Right, a murdered relative was so unseemly. Whatever would people think? "Well, were Gordon and Darren close?"

"Darren and Gordon were good friends once they became adults. They skied together and went to the club sometimes. They weren't as close as Gordon and I were, but they were solid. With eight years between them, it took a long time for them to be on the same footing, if you understand what I mean. They had little in common as a ten-year-old and an eighteen-year-old. The difference was less significant once they were in their twenties and thirties, all grown up as they say. And, of course, they worked together, too."

"What kind of work did they do?"

"They played the stock market, financial planning and investments, that kind of thing. Darren still handles all the portfolios for their clients."

"Would you mind if I talked with Darren?"

"Of course not."

"What's the best way to reach him?"

"If you give it half an hour, you can find him at Pockets. It's a billiard club at Spadina and Wellington. He plays there every afternoon from about two till four or five. He calls the place his second office."

The broker with the pool cue in the billiard hall? What next? Colonel Mustard in the conservatory with the candlestick? If Darren went there every day, his business had to either be doing exceptionally well or exceptionally poorly.

"I guess I'm headed there next. Thank you. And I know it doesn't mean much, but I'm sorry for your loss."

"Thank you. Would you like to come to Chadwick's and see the new summer line? The distributor always brings several testers and demo products."

"Nah. I'll finish my coffee and then head down to Pockets." But not till I'd emptied and filled my own pockets.

*On my mark, get set, go.* I ran a block down the street to an office supplies store and copied the contents of Rebecca's wallet. I placed all the business cards, receipts, dry-cleaning slips — everything — face down on the photocopier. Then I did the same with the credit cards and ID.

I might burn in hell some day, but I'd have an interesting time on my journey there.

A few minutes later warm black-and-white copies were stuffed in my pocket, and the wallet looked just as it had when I'd pilfered it. I detoured by the shop and told Rebecca she must have dropped it.

"Why, thank you. I never even noticed."

That was the point.

# Tuesday, 2:20 p.m.

"Hi, I'm looking for Darren. Is he around?"

The bored dude at the counter tilted his head in the direction of the green felt table at the back of the room.

The two words that leaped to mind when I saw Darren were *ruddy* and *stubby*, almost the complete opposite of his translucent, sylphlike sister. His face had the flushed colouring of someone who drank a lot or spent a lot of time at sea. Since it was April, and Toronto's sailing season was still in the offing, I was guessing the former. He was a nice enough looking guy, not exactly short, but at five foot nine and probably a hundred and eighty pounds, he was never going to be considered eye candy.

His opponent, a tall slender Asian kid of about seventeen, missed his shot, and Darren was now chalking up. Not wanting to interrupt Darren in mid-game, I sat at the counter and ordered a Coke.

Although Rebecca had referred to the place as a billiard club, seedy pool hall was more like it. It displayed every stereotype of the dimly lit rooms shown in gangster flicks. The concession stand sold potato chips and chocolate bars that had probably been packaged in the 1980s. A deep fryer stood at the ready for a range of artery-clogging delicacies like French fries and chicken wings, should anyone have the courage to order. They had two kinds of draft beer, flat or watered-down, plus a slim selection of bottled beers.

I pumped some quarters into a video game and sipped my Coke right out of the can. I had some serious misgivings about the sterility of the glassware. A second later I just about spit out my swig of cola when I heard a spew of venom erupt from the table where Darren was playing.

"No fucking way, you slanty-eyed asshole," Darren snarled. "You didn't fucking call that fucking shot."

"What did you just call me? Fuck you, I ain't no slanty-eye, you racist prick."

"Yeah, well, your eyesight can't be too fucking good if you can't tell a bank-left-side, corner-pocket shot from that fucking fluke you just hit. Game's over, dude. Pony up the dough."

"Bullshit, fuckface. That's what I called. You gotta pay me. A hundred bucks, man. Now."

"In a pig's eye, fucking cheater."

I turned to the still-bored-looking guy at the counter. "What the heck's going on over there?"

"The usual. Darren's a sore loser and the other guy's a hustler. Same shit, different day. Shouldn't bet if ya aren't willing to say *adiós* to the cash, and Darren can't stand losing."

*Thwack!*

Darren's pool cue was now in two pieces. The Asian guy threw them both onto the floor. Darren picked that moment to up the ante and sucker-punched him in the face.

"That was a customized cue, you fucking piece of rice-eating shit." His fist was about to reconnect with the other guy's jaw when Bored Counter Guy stepped between them.

"Out of here! Now! Both of you!"

The young Asian dude took his jacket from the peg on the wall and marched out with his head held high. Good for you, I thought. Darren started to argue with Bored Guy, saying he had no right to bar him from the establishment. "This fucking place would go out of business if it weren't for me."

"Chill out, Darren. You're not barred. Just don't talk to people like that. Go and cool off and I'll see you tomorrow."

Darren's behaviour told me all I needed to know about him. Hot-tempered, narrow-minded bigot. I'd seen enough for now. I abandoned my can of Coke and left.

And why did a financial planner spend all afternoon in a pool hall, anyway? In theory I could see it as a place to mix business and pleasure, but if that were the case this pool hall was the wrong fit. I could see it in a classy joint with antique tables and a selection of single-malt Scotches served by svelte waitresses in snug black miniskirts, but not in a place with cans of Coke and servers named Bubba.

# Tuesday, 4:00 p.m.

I had time to kill before my night job, and I was hungry. So I did what I usually did when I wanted to eat and didn't want to cook. I walked the several blocks north to "restaurant row" on Elm Street. My wonderful brother, Shane, was chef extraordinaire and indentured servant-slash-partner at Pastiche, one of Toronto's trendier dining rooms.

Like an embarrassing and unwanted stepchild, I bypassed the main entrance and walked through the laneway to the back. I banged on the kitchen door, which was usually reserved for staff, deliveries, or hungry sisters.

"Yo, bro, what's tonight's special?"

"Hey, I've got something new. Grab a seat and tell me what you think."

Shane assembled a plate for me, and I sat at the scarred side table next to the walk-in fridge. Prep cooks were busy slicing and dicing, the dishwasher was polishing silverware, and wait staff were milling in and out of the kitchen, all of them anticipating the evening's dinner rush.

Delicious food: ten; atmosphere: zero. But since I often ate here free, I couldn't complain, even if I was eating in a hot and noisy kitchen. Since Shane and his partner had opened Pastiche a few months ago, reservations had been booked solid and showed no signs of slowing down.

"My God, this is good! What is it?" I was talking with my mouth full, but I didn't care.

Shane beamed as he always did when he served one of his new creations. "Lobster truffle risotto. How are the spices?"

"Very, very good. Needs a bit more salt, but perfect texture."

"Great! We're offering it as the first course on our prix-fixe menu tonight. Save some room. I want you to try my other creation — pan-seared bison tenderloin with chanterelles and stewed apples."

"I won't be able to move. Just give me a small portion."

As Shane prepared my plate, I told him about my day.

"You're what?"

"Investigating a murder. Not just any murder, but Gordon Hanes. Remember last summer, the Rosedale silver-spoon who was shot in the ravine off Rosedale Valley Road?"

"Oh, yeah. But how did you get involved?"

I filled him in on Christine's visit to my office. "She Googled Toronto private investigators and found me. I guess she checked some others, too. She told me she chose me because I'm cheap."

"Unbelievable. That's why people like her have so much money. They're so unwilling to part with it. So what else?"

I told Shane about the visit with Rebecca, the purse, the pills, the wallet, and her sniffling, and then about Darren, the bigot with the broken cue.

"Shit. Sounds like you just got a walk-on role in a low-budget soap opera."

"Tell me about it."

We chatted for a few minutes longer and then I took his hint to leave. The restaurant opened its doors at five o'clock, and Shane had to get back to work.

"Thanks for dinner. The bison thing is sure to sell out." Nothing beat a free gourmet dinner with a nice guy who wasn't trying to hit on me.

# Tuesday, 8:56 p.m.

"Oh. Yeah. Baby." My voice held about as much sexual excitement as a Jersey cow being milked.

My rock and roll days were pretty much over. A couple of years ago, as my thirtieth birthday approached, I'd finally admitted that setting the world on fire as a kick-ass singer wasn't likely to happen. Corporate gigs, weddings, neighbourhood bars, and local fairs were never going to catapult me to the top of *Billboard*'s charts. I walked away from the music business and now only toyed with it as a hobby, or when good friends hooked me up with a show.

A singer didn't really have a lot of transferable skills. Belting out rock tunes and swivelling my hips would never translate into an office job. Pushing thirty, I realized the best I could do with my biggest asset — my voice — was sporadic radio voice-overs, which paid crap, or occasionally interesting but slimy phone sex calls, which paid very well. At least the "1-900-I'm–a-wanker-and-can't-get-my-rocks-off-any-other-way" job offered flex hours, and I could read or surf the Net while faking an orgasm. The job had paid my college tuition and was now keeping me afloat while I tried to establish myself as a sleuth.

The man on the other end of the phone sounded like a sweaty, hairy, blue-collar Star Trekkie. "Tell me how badly you want it. Beg me for it."

Another hour and this shift would thankfully be over. I peeled my eyes away from the computer screen in front of me and injected a kittenish purr into my voice. "*Oooohhh* … yeah, hot stuff, I want it *baaaad* … I want you …"

*I want you to hang up, go away, far, far away, and spend your days as a nomad high in the Andes, far removed from the wonders of telecommunications.*

The pervert continued. "Beg me for it, baby. Tell me what it's gonna feel like."

I could hear the rancid sweatiness in his voice. I played along with his fantasy. "Stop teasing me and start pleasing me," I cooed. "*Oooh* ... yeah ... I'm trembling, I'm tingling ..."

I was cringing, more like it. I went on autopilot, telling the loser on the line what he wanted to hear. The men were all the same — *beg me for it, make me feel virile and sexy like the stud muffin I am* — because, God knows, a truly hot piece of eye candy would have nothing better to do with his evenings than get his rocks off calling a phone sex line. Yeah, right.

I continued purring and moaning, peppered with a few dirty words and some X-rated phrases as I surfed the Internet. A bunch of old news stories about Gordon Hanes's murder came up. A few articles gave brief comments from friends and family; some had interviews with people close to him. Mostly, they just gave the basic facts of who, what, when, and where, but of course none told me why and that was what I wanted to know most of all.

The stories all said the same thing. On Saturday, July 5, 2008, at approximately 9:15 a.m., the body of Gordon Hanes was discovered in the Rosedale Valley ravine by a couple of cyclists. The cyclists had a cell phone and called 911. Police and an ambulance arrived in about five minutes.

The victim was pronounced dead on the scene, a result of the three bullet holes in his back — one in his ass, the other two through his left shoulder blade. He'd been dead about two or three hours when officials arrived.

Although the murder occurred in a relatively open area, no one saw or heard anything — surprise, surprise. The heavily treed ravine ran below the Bloor Viaduct, a busy bridge, heavy with traffic even on a Saturday, and even noisier given the subway train below it. The Don Valley Parkway was parallel to the ravine, and it, too, was packed with cars and trucks all day, every day. And alongside it were the rails for the GO commuter trains serving the outer reaches of the greater Toronto area. If anyone had heard anything, they'd probably assumed it was a car backfiring or the usual grunting of the trains.

Law-enforcement officials had put yellow crime scene tape around the area and had searched for whatever it was police search for when a corpse turned up. They had questioned joggers, cyclists, and dog walkers, all to no avail. Eventually, they found the weapon, an unregistered illegal handgun that was traced back to New York State but no further. The mayor got on his soapbox again about the influx of illegal firearms from the United States as the cause of Toronto's gun crime, deftly putting the blame for the city's crime rate on someone else's shoulders.

The murder got a lot of media coverage, and a 1-800 phone line was set up to receive anonymous tips. Nothing. A reward was offered. Nothing came of that. The story kept getting news coverage. Still no arrests. Christine seemed to be the odds-on favourite as the culprit, but investigators found nothing to connect her to the crime, even after a thorough investigation.

Eventually, the news reports all started to say the same nothing: "Police are pursuing several leads ... the investigations is still open ... no comment ... we can't discuss an ongoing investigation ..." and so on.

Some heavy panting in my ear brought me back to reality. The horny schmuck on the phone was on the brink of physical gratification and needed dirty talk from me to guide him through it. Twenty more minutes to go. I trotted out everything I'd learned about performing and guided Sweaty-Hairy-Trekkie to tele-comm-tele-cum.

# Wednesday, April 8, 10:30 a.m.

I had already seen the two cousins; now it was time to meet the woman from whose loins Gordon had sprung. I was sensitive enough to Gordon's grieving mother to give more thought about how I'd handle her. I didn't think the psychology student story would carry me very far.

I was sitting in the living room of the Riverdale home I shared with my often absent dad and Shane, who was still sleeping. Dad was off on one of his extended trips. He'd bought himself a camper van after retiring as a math professor at the University of Toronto. For the past six years he'd spent the winters honing his card-shark skills as he travelled through whatever U.S. states had casinos. In summer Dad cast his line from the deck of our cabin cruiser in Upstate New York. Fishing in the Thousand Islands was the only thing that eclipsed games of chance and probability for his attention.

It was good that he was gone for extended periods because it made it easy to hide things from him, like my phone sex job. He didn't need to know about that.

I stared out the living-room window for a few minutes, not really seeing anything. I was trying to get my story straight in my head, and attempting to get my head on straight since I hadn't had a coffee yet. When I sorted out a makeshift script, I went into the kitchen, turned on the coffee maker, and called Mrs. Hanes.

"Hello." A woman with a small voice answered.

"Hi, my name is Sasha Jackson, and I'm a freelance writer. May I please speak with Maureen Hanes?"

"This is she."

"I'm doing an article on unsolved homicides in Toronto." No beating around the bush for little old me. "I'd like to follow up on the death of your son."

Freelance writer seemed as good a bullshit cover as anything else. Hell, if I could fake orgasms in a call centre with fluorescent lights, I could fake just about anything. I only hoped she didn't ask to see any of my published work. I heard a soft sigh on the other end of the phone line.

"What can I do for you?"

"I'd like some background about Gordon. Biographical. It's really a human-interest piece. You know, give some dimension to the victim. Most people just remember the headlines, but they forget the person."

"I see. Yes, sadly that's true." She sighed again.

The woman appeared either defeated or disinterested, but she hadn't told me to buzz off, so I tried to tug the heartstrings.

"It's been many months and no one has been charged. It looks like the case has gone cold, as they say. And it shouldn't. Gordon deserves to be remembered. My angle is the family and friends who miss him, what the loss means to them and how they've coped."

"I see. Perhaps it's best if we talk in person. Why don't you come by the house?"

---

The house, though only a few miles from mine, was worlds away. The Tudor-style Rosedale home with picture windows and a three-car garage had old money written all over it. Even in the muddy cusp of spring the grounds were flawless. A few crocuses were just beginning to bud next to the white gravel walkway that led to the door.

As soon as I met Mrs. Hanes, I realized that what I'd taken for apathy on the phone was, in fact, her whole personality. It seemed as if loneliness had coloured her world; everything from her nondescript hairdo to her ecru blouse, taupe skirt, and apricot lipstick screamed boring. I was as out of place here as I had been yesterday when I breached the gold-plated gates of Yorkville.

I hadn't dressed up for that visit because that wasn't my thing, but the trip to Rosedale called for better than my usual faded, low-slung Levis and T-shirt. I'd decided on urban chic, which to me meant my good jeans, sans worn-out knees or frayed bottoms, and a fitted red shirt with a wraparound waist. The moisture in the spring air meant my hair was in full-scale rebellion, so I'd pinned it into something that resembled either a chignon or an eagle's nest piled high on top of my head.

"A pleasure to meet you, but I'm sorry it's because of such a sad subject." I stuck out my hand, and she replied by offering a cold bony thing that belonged in the grocer's frozen fish aisle.

"Please come in. I have tea ready in the den."

I followed her into the uninspired room and sat on a dull mushroom-coloured leather sofa. The upholstery was as supple as butter, and it was clearly worth more than I'd earn in a year, yet it was as drab as the woman herself.

"Things just haven't been the same since Gordon died."

She poured some tepid Earl Grey into plain white teacups. They were bone china, of course, expensive but innocuous, like everything else about the woman and her home. I longed for a shot of Grand Marnier to put a little zing into the tea, and maybe into the forthcoming conversation, as well.

I began. "I can't imagine the void you must have in your life now that Gordon's gone."

"He was an only child. I have nothing now. My husband died of prostrate cancer five years ago."

It would have seemed callous to correct *prostate*.

"That must have been very hard to cope with. What about other relatives?"

"Well, there's my sister, Lucille, and her family, of course. She has a son and daughter I'm very fond of. But it's not the same. I'll get to watch my niece and nephew live their lives, but I won't get to do that with my son. They'll marry and start their families. I'll be a doting great-aunt, but I'll never be a doting grandmother." She took a sip of tea, then sighed and put the cup down. She looked at me and waited for me to continue.

"I guess you must sometimes wonder what would have happened if Gordon and Christine had married, after all."

"Christine was such a nice girl."

What? First indication of this ... At my office Christine had been rude, pretentious, and impatient. And from my visit with Rebecca, it seemed she felt the same way about Christine.

"I really don't believe she killed him, but many people do think so." She set her cup down and waited for my reply.

"With the whole spurned-lover thing, I can see why they'd think that. But if she didn't do it, then who do you think did?"

"It's easier to believe it was a random killing, that he was in the wrong place at the wrong time. Then I don't have to wrap my head around some horrible secret truth that would be a reason for someone wanting him dead."

"Why don't you tell me what he was like, what made him tick?" I opened the notebook I had brought with me and started taking notes.

"Well, he was popular, a real social butterfly. He had a zest for life and was really keen about everything. He took a strong interest in his friends, his hobbies, in whatever he was doing. Gordon was always the life of the party."

So the complete opposite of you, I thought to myself. Grief-stricken or not, I couldn't picture this woman ever having a belly laugh.

"Who was he closest to besides family?"

"Well, Ted Chapman was his best friend, right from about the time they first met in elementary school. And he had a group of golfing buddies. They played locally whenever they could and did two or three golf trips a year. Usually Myrtle Beach, but two summers ago they did St. Andrews. That was special to him. Gordon had always wanted to go there. I'm so glad he had the chance to do that. Let me get my photo albums. There's a really nice picture of him at the eighteenth hole."

She spent the next hour showing me a photorama of Gordon's whole life. I saw the buck-toothed teenybopper before braces, the high-school jock with train tracks on his teeth, and the graduate, sans metal work, with a smile his orthodontist could use as a testimonial.

"And here he is at New Year's 2004, it says. That's his friend Ted there." She pointed to an incredibly handsome, tall, broad-shouldered guy with wavy sandy hair. "I can't remember this other boy's name, and this one here in the blue shirt is his cousin Darren."

It was a typical New Year's Eve party photo. There were dashes of colour from the curlicues of serpentines and streamers strewn throughout the room. The photo seemed semi-candid, since Gordon was looking off to the side of the room and Darren — a champagne magnum in hand — blinked as the picture was taken. Or maybe he'd just passed out standing up.

"Maybe I should talk with Ted. You said he was Gordon's best friend?"

"I can call ahead and let him know you'll be in touch with him."

If Ted looked anything like his picture, I'd rather touch him than just be in touch …

## *Wednesday, 12:30 p.m.*

Handsome, perfect male specimen or not, I wasn't in the mood to talk with another blueblood right away. I was still curious about Darren, not just because he was an asshole, but I wondered how a stockbroker could spend so much time away from the office. So I called up my source for all things financial.

"Mr. Belham, I was wondering if I could drop by and talk with you for a few minutes?"

Mr. Belham, grand poobah of The Belham Group, was one of my first clients when I graduated. He ran an investment public-relations and marketing firm and had hired me to do background checks on two potential new employees. One of them turned out to have a very shady past and a forged M.B.A., so I think he was now flipping burgers somewhere. The other candidate was a great guy and had pulled himself up and out of a very disadvantaged upbringing on the wrong side of the tracks. I had always rooted for the underdog, so I was glad when my snooping on him didn't uncover any dirt.

"Is this about one of our hires?" Belham asked.

"No. Actually, it's sort of personal. I just need some information. It has nothing to do with corporate hiring. Can I drop by? I'm just a couple of blocks away."

"I'm about to head into a meeting. I have some time at 2:30, though, if that suits you."

"Perfect. See you then."

I had about two hours to kill. I didn't see the point in going home, as I'd just have to turn around and come back. It was sunny and mild, so I decided to hang around downtown. I stopped at a bank machine and deposited the cheque Christine had given me, then I walked up to Steve's on Queen Street and immediately fell in love.

Steve's was probably the best musical instrument store in Toronto, and I sometimes avoided going there because I either spent way more than I could afford or got depressed because I'd exercised restraint and not bought all the cool stuff on display.

I'd wanted to upgrade my drum set for a while, and Steve's had a totally kickass Mapex set on display that I'd have given my first-born child for. And my second- and third-born, as well. Singing had always been my strength, and I had a natural talent for it, but for pure enjoyment, give me a set of drums any day. There was just something so sexy about being able to whack the shit out of something and calling it art.

"Hey, Sasha, why don't you give them a try? You're practically drooling." Hutch, the salesclerk, knew me well from my visits over the years.

"No way, Hutch. I'm just killing time. Can't afford anything these days." Even though the cheque from Christine would take a few days to clear, the money from it was already spent.

"Check it out, Sash. It's on sale." At eighteen hundred it was a deal, but about seventeen hundred more than I could spare.

"Hutch, you're like a crack dealer. You know, *'c'mon, just try it, it won't hurt you, you can stop anytime.'* The next thing I know, I'm hooked and stealing welfare checks from single moms to support my music addiction."

"Eight-coat, hand-rubbed lacquer finishes. Weather-king drumheads." The set was fully loaded, with a twenty-two-inch bass, three tom drums, a snare, cymbals, and all the bells-and-whistles hardware. "You could use our layaway plan."

Hutch knew more about instruments and making music than most people ever would. He also knew his customers and how to finesse them, and for that reason I alternately loved and hated him.

"Man, you suck. Gimme the sticks, Hutch."

I tapped away for a minute, and then gave in to temptation and let it all out. I banged on the drums as if it were the last chance I'd ever have to play. A few customers turned to watch, but in a music store that wasn't so unusual. What was unusual — to most people — was a chick drummer. I figured guys were both threatened and entranced by a girl who liked hitting things so hard. During my band days, I'd stuck to singing, which I was pretty damn good at, but drums had always been my passion, and I would have killed to have been able to make a career out of playing them.

The Mapex set's sound was excellent; the feeling I got from playing such perfect equipment was heady. The self-restraint I exhibited in the face of Hutch's sales pitch was a first for me. I'd get a new set eventually, but there was no way I could afford it right now.

"Let me see how work goes in the next while, and if I can afford them, I'll be back."

Daydreaming about the percussion equivalent of the shirtless fireman on the cover of last year's calendar, I trotted back down to King Street and up to the fifty-seventh-floor office of Mr. Belham. His bald head, horn-rimmed glasses, and ill-fitting suit snapped me out of La La Land and into the pinstriped world of Bay Street finance.

We went through a few minutes of routine social pleasantries before I got to my point. "Do you know the Hanes family or the Blackmores? Rosedale folks from way back?"

"I'm familiar with them, yes. Why do you ask?"

"Well, sir ..." I was pretty sure I'd never called anyone else "sir," but Belham commanded that kind of respect. "I'm looking into the murder of Gordon Hanes, and a few things make me wonder about his cousin Darren Blackmore. I thought since he's in investments, too, you might be able to tell me a bit about him. Or Gordon."

"I would prefer not to indulge in gossip."

"I'd never dream of asking you to. Just tell me what you know, if you can. Maybe the family business history?"

"The family money comes from the mother's side. Maureen and her sister, Lucille, inherited a fortune when their father died. He made his money the same way — from his inheritance. The great-grandfather started it all, back in the days when motorized cars first came on the scene. The old man — what was his name? Oxford? Yes, Emery Oxford started the first taxicab company in Toronto. He also owned the first few corner gas stations. He leased out the taxis and made them sign an exclusive agreement to buy their petrol at his stations. This kind of monopoly would hardly be legal nowadays, but back then it was."

"Interesting. What else?"

"The next generation diversified a bit. They did some real-estate development, as I recall, but mainly they stuck to related industries. Shipping and transport. Nothing sensational."

"I guess if it ain't broke, why fix it."

"Precisely. Then in the late fifties, with the dawn of suburbia and shopping malls and the new consumerism, the family got into fast-food restaurants of all things."

"Really? That seems so beneath them. Kind of bourgeois."

"Perhaps, but the bottom line was the important thing. They owned several burger franchises, all in excellent locations. They still do. The family isn't hands-on these days, but the money from hamburgers and milk shakes has given them a very nice life indeed."

"Indeed."

"After they married, Maureen's husband, William Hanes, very consciously moved them to less pedestrian enterprises, namely investment and finance. And then their son and his cousin Darren took over when the elder generation stepped down."

"I saw Darren yesterday. I wasn't with him, but we were both at a pool hall downtown. Seems like a hothead. He got into a fight with another player, and it got kind of ugly."

"That's not too surprising. Darren is mercurial. He can be charming, and he's quite extroverted. But Darren has gotten a rather sour reputation in the past couple of years. He drinks a fair bit and is unpleasant to be around when he's been imbibing."

"I don't think he'd been drinking yesterday, at least not very much, but, man, what a mouth on him, and what a temper."

"He's a rather unpredictable fellow and can be volatile. That's for certain. He made quite a bit of noise a year or two ago. The Ontario Securities Commission had some questions about some of his investment transactions."

Now that piqued my interest. "Really? What happened?"

"I never knew all the details."

"So what came of it?"

"As they say, the best defence is a good offence. Darren was quite belligerent and aggressive when they asked him about some of his dealings. I remember he threatened libel or slander, something like that. Then it just seemed to die down."

"Wow! Do you think any of that could be related to Gordon's murder?"

"I suppose it's possible, but I think it's unlikely. Other than that one incident a while back, their reputations are fine. And Gordon's name was never actually associated with that nasty business, anyway."

"Well, sir, this is a lot to think about. Thank you."

"My pleasure."

"You've been very helpful, but I don't want to take any more of you time. I'll see myself out."

"I'll be in touch in a couple of months when we recruit again."

So Darren had some tarnish on his sterling-silver surliness. He had struck me as such an asshole that I wondered fleetingly if maybe someone had killed the wrong cousin.

Next up: the victim's best friend, Ted, he of the broad shoulders and wavy sandy hair. Maybe he could shed some light on the personalities involved. I was curious to hear what someone outside the family had to say about the Hanes clan.

# *Wednesday, 4:00 p.m.*

"**I** could use an hour away from my desk," Ted Chapman told me over the phone. "How about the bar at Tundra?"

*Yikes!* The prices there were astronomical. "Perfect. I'm on my way." At least my good jeans and red shirt were borderline acceptable for the slick chrome-and-mirrored watering hole of choice among poseurs with more money than sense. I hoped I passed for a Yuppie slumming it.

While Tundra might be cool, Ted was very hot. He was better-looking than in the photo. About six foot two and solid, without looking like an overzealous bodybuilder who drank raw egg protein shakes. The sandy hair was a bit shorter and less wavy, but still had the tousled look to it. The smile was as delicious as I'd expected from the old photo and made me think of gumdrops. Yum. Gumdrops?

"I'm going to have a single malt. Would you care for one?" He was standing at the bar and had his gold card out, so I figured he was buying and said yes.

"Two thirty-year-old Cregneash, neat, please." He signed for our drinks and then steered us to a table by the window. "Cheers," he said.

"*Sláinte.*" Gaelic, I'm told, for "Cheers."

I noticed there was no ring on the finger, not that that necessarily meant anything. I had to remind myself not to flirt; I was meeting him under false pretenses. Mrs. Hanes had called ahead and told him to expect to hear from a journalist writing about her dead son, though she probably hadn't put it that way.

Ted looked right at me as he spoke. I tried to pay attention, but kept noticing his eyes and his perfect white teeth.

"Gordie was a good friend. I still really miss him."

"I'm sure you do. It must be especially hard when it's a violent death and no one's been punished for it."

"Well ... yes, it is. It's hard not to be bitter and resentful of the justice system. I'm not a cop or a lawyer, but it's certainly hard not to second-guess their investigation."

"What do you mean?"

"Well, it seems to me they should have looked harder at Christine. She was a queen bee at times and could really fly off the handle. When Gordon ended their engagement, she had a fit. I wasn't there, but he told me about it. She slapped him, ran through a list of four-letter words, and said she'd make him regret the decision."

"I'm sure it wasn't pretty. I'm not excusing her, but doesn't that reaction seem normal for a fiancée who's just been dumped? Knee-jerk emotions and all that?"

"Maybe ..."

We sat in silence for a moment, each of us sipping our dram of silky firewater, the smoothest Scotch I'd ever tasted.

"It just seems too weird that he was killed on the day they were supposed to get married."

I just about spat my decades-old single malt all over the bevelled glass table. "What?"

"You didn't know? I think the police ignored it, and to me it was significant. He was killed on Saturday, July 5, the exact date they'd planned for their wedding."

*How come no one told me that? Holy shit!*

"It just seems too much of a coincidence," Ted continued. "But the police questioned her and didn't have anything to go on, I guess. She was off as usual at the mother-daughter thing in Cobourg she does every month with her mom."

"Unbelievable. I met his cousin Rebecca, and she sort of hinted that maybe Christine had a hand in things. Rebecca made it seem like it was a contract killing or something. I didn't know that about the date, though. Makes more sense now."

"Well, it does sound kind of far-fetched. I mean, how do you recruit a killer? But Christine has money, and in this city, anything's possible for the right price."

Man, if this really was murder for hire, then I was in way over my head. And if Christine came from money, then — my stellar services notwithstanding — why was I all she could afford? "That puts a whole new light on things," I said to Ted.

I figured it was time to shelve the murder questions if I wanted to be convincing about my human-interest, don't-forget-the-victim journalism angle, so I got back to my real fake purpose of meeting Ted. "Tell me a bit more about Gordon. What was he like?"

"He was a lot of fun, but he could be rigid. He had set routines and didn't like to veer from them. When it was time to have fun, he really did, but he was very focused, too. You know, like they say, work hard, play hard."

"What did he do for fun?"

"He was really into sports. Went jogging every morning without fail. Golf in summer, skiing in winter. He really liked swimming and water sports, too. I have a family cottage up north, and Gordon loved to hang out there and go water skiing."

I got a mental visual of Ted in swimming trunks. *Zowie!* "Was Christine interested in sports, too?"

"She's not very outdoorsy. She'd come along sometimes, but she'd just sit and watch. She prefers cultural activities, like theatre and galleries, that kind of thing. When they started dating, Gordon really seemed to compartmentalize things. Friday nights with the boys, Saturday nights with her, Tuesdays to the movies with her. Wednesday was hockey with the guys. She never got on well with any of the other guys' girlfriends. I guess that's why he kept that part of his life separate."

Time for me to do a little fishing. "What does your girlfriend think of her?"

"I don't have one."

*Goody, goody, goody.*

Ted continued. "Actually, I did see a girl for a while, Denise, and she met Christine once when we were all at the same party. It's funny how women are, you know?"

*Oh, God, don't start talking to me like I'm one of the boys.* I decided I should unpin the hair and let it fall onto my shoulders, but had no idea how to do that without seeming obvious. Ditto for undoing the top two buttons on my blouse. Damn! *Hey, sexy guy, notice me, notice me!*

"Uh, yeah," I said, "I'm familiar with the fairer sex ..."

"Sorry, you know what I mean. We were all at this party, and the girls met each other and chatted away nicely for a while. They talked about clothes or something and seemed to hit it off. When we left, Christine and Denise were saying we'd all have to get together sometime for dinner or drinks. Air kisses on each other's cheeks when we said good night. Then, in the car, not two seconds later, Denise told me what she really thought of Christine. Said she was a pretentious bitch."

"You can't tell me you didn't agree, though."

"I did agree, but what turned me off was the hypocrisy and immediate backstabbing. It was a complete and instant about-face. I mean, Denise didn't know at that point what I thought of Christine. Suppose Christine and I had been good friends or something? And here Denise was calling Christine a pretentious bitch, which by then was pretty much what I thought of Denise, so that was our last date."

I wasn't good at the whole feminine wiles-flirty thing. I was only half listening to what he was saying, letting my mind wander instead to what the size of his penis might be. He had big hands and his fingers were long and broad …

My stage persona, back in my rocker chick days, could pull off shameless flirting. But that was an act, an over-the-top one at that, and it was expected. When I was singing, it was okay to get a little crazy and go wild with the whole teasing, sex appeal thing. In real life I couldn't play the mating game without getting tongue-tied and feeling stupid, unless you counted the phone sex gig, which was too twisted to guide me in real-life situations. Maybe telepathy would work. This guy gave me butterflies in a way no guy had since time immemorial, or at least since my last relationship, which I'd done my very best to forget. I gave myself a mental head shake and forced myself back into the comfort zone of investigator working a case.

Raising my glass, I said, "Well, here's to Christine and Denise. May they end up at the same hoity-toity, black-tie event, wearing the exact same one-of-a-kind designer dress."

Ted laughed and clinked his glass with mine.

I continued. "It kind of seems odd they were a couple, doesn't it? Christine sounds so different from Gordon." I couldn't picture the two of them together. Then again, the only guy I could see putting up with Little Miss My-Shit-Doesn't-Stink would have to be deaf and mute.

"Oh, Christine can turn on the charm when she wants to, and really, she does have her good points. They had some common bonds — same clubs, a couple of fundraising events. Their parents were acquainted with one another. Sorry if this sounds elitist, but they kind of moved in the same circles."

"What does Christine do? I can't imagine her holding down a job."

Ted chuckled. "No, she's definitely not the workaday kind of girl. She's an art dealer. Her family owns a couple of galleries. One in the Queen's Quay Terminal at Harbourfront and the other at Hazelton Lanes."

A waitress appeared out of nowhere with another round of Scotch for us. Ted and I clinked glasses again.

"I never would have pictured her in a field like that," I said. "What kind of art?"

"The Queen's Quay gallery deals in Inuit art. It's mostly sculpture, stone, or whalebone carvings and that kind of Canadiana. That probably does well with all the tourists who go to that area. It has a lot of landscape paintings, too, I think."

"I bet it does. 'Gotta get that soapstone carving as a keepsake of the trip to Canada.'"

"You got it. I'm not sure about the other gallery. I think it has a range of unknown contemporary artists, mostly locals."

I was already feeling the effects of the Scotch. The shots they poured here were very generous. I hoped I wasn't slurring my words at all.

"What kind of background does Christine have for this?" I could have easily found this out. It was my forte, after all, but I was enjoying the eye candy and was in no hurry to end the meeting. I wondered what it would be like to accidentally fall on Ted's penis …

"I know she studied out west — Simon Fraser University or maybe the University of British Columbia. Not sure which. I just know she did art history. You should probably give Christine a call. She could really help you with your article. She experienced a loss, too, even if they weren't actually a couple when he died."

*Oh, yeah, right. I'm a freelance writer or something like that. Human-interest piece about a victim. Got it.*

"That's a good suggestion, Ted. It probably would be helpful to talk to her."

"I can get you her contact info."

"How about if I just give you my number and you pass it on?" But not before making note of my cell number yourself, handsome. Powers of suggestion: do your damnedest.

I gave Ted one of the ultra-basic business cards I always carried. It had my name, Sasha Jackson, my cell number, and my Hotmail address on it — and nothing else. The one-size-fits-all business card came in handy when picking up guys or trying to, and when scooping up clients. When I first started working for myself, I ordered business cards with a cute little magnifying glass and deerstalker cap logo and the title PRIVATE INVESTIGATOR under my name. On the rare occasions soon after, if I happened to meet an eligible, attractive man, he was immediately scared off as soon as he read my business card. I guess no guy wanted to date under a microscope. So I had downgraded the cards. It was probably immaterial, anyway. At that point in my life I wasn't really ready to date; the scars from my last broken heart hadn't yet healed. Memories of Mick flashed through my brain for a second, but I immediately snapped out of that dysfunctional trip down memory lane and focused on the beefcake with a brain sitting across the table from me.

"By the way, did Gordon meet anyone or do any dating after they split up?" I asked.

"Not really. I set him up on a date with one of the women who works in the same office building as I do. They went out a couple times, but apparently neither of them felt there was any spark."

## Wednesday, 7:30 p.m.

My best friend Lindsey and I were sitting at the bar at the Pilot Tavern, our favourite pisstank. Our friend Jessica was bartending at a function upstairs in the Stealth Lounge, the private party room at the Pilot, or we would have sat in her section.

Lindsey signalled for another round before she spoke. Derrick, the bartender, poured us a couple of pints of

Strongbow cider, and we were all set up for a gabfest. We hadn't talked in a couple of days, and brought each other up to speed.

"Oh, yeah, there was a spark all right," I said after describing my meeting with Ted Chapman. "But there's no way I can go there, at least not right now. I lied to him about who I am and what I do. He thinks I'm a writer doing a story on how family and friends cope with violent deaths, or something like that. Not the best way to get a relationship off the ground."

"You could bend the truth a whole lot and say this is your first article ... keep flirting with him till you win him over."

"Like you did with Shane?"

"Touché."

Lindsey's real name was Lakshmi, a name she'd hated since her family came to Canada from Sri Lanka when she was four years old. Lindsey wasn't only my best friend; she was also my brother's girlfriend, something she'd hoped for as a pimply-faced teen. It had taken them more than a decade to get together, and it would probably take just as long to get them to the altar.

In earlier days they were never on the same page. As a gawky sixteen-year-old, my brother had wanted nothing to do with his kid sister's flat-chested friend. Then, in university, once Lindsey had blossomed, she'd had a severe bout of cultural identity conflict and gone back to using her Hindu birth name and dating only South Asian guys. As Lindsey/Lakshmi had gotten older, she'd wanted to know more about her roots and culture, but having been raised in Canada she'd found it hard to identify with South Asian culture.

Most of the traditional Sri Lankan men she'd dated had values and expectations instilled by mothers still steeped in the ways of the old country. Lindsey could never and would never embrace the beliefs and gender roles that some East Indian guys expected of her, and her lackadaisical religious views were appalling to more than a few potential suitors. Lindsey had eventually realized she was North American through and through, Indo-Pakistani packaging notwithstanding. By the time she'd come to terms with her dual identity, Shane was out of the country, exploring other cultures himself.

Shane had spent a few years in Europe apprenticing in some really upscale kitchens, mostly in Spain and Italy. He'd learned from some of the very best chefs and had become a master of fusion cuisine. The jobs abroad were all part of his long-range plan to open his own upscale *bôite* someday. At his welcome-back-to-Toronto party, about two years ago, Shane and Lindsey had finally gotten together after a lot of alcohol and some not-so-subtle pushing from me. From grappa to grabbing in six easy shooters. The question now was: how long would it take for them to tie the knot? Each of them seemed so wrapped up in their respective career that a wedding didn't seem in the offing ... for now.

"Okay, so then what do you think of the Christine chick?" Lindsey asked. "Sounds to me like she's the prime suspect, as they say."

"Yeah, it would seem. Except a few things bother me."

"Like what?"

"Well, why would she hire me for one thing?"

"Because you're not very good, and have zero experience with this kind of thing, so it's safe to assume you'll find out a big fat nothing?"

"Thanks a bunch," I said. "If I didn't need self-esteem therapy before, I sure do now. Actually, speaking of therapy, want to go to a chi-chi-spa-yoga-wheat-germ retreat this weekend?"

"You're kidding, right?"

"No, seriously. It's a holier-than-thou-wellness-and-vanity place in Cobourg. Christine was there the weekend Gordon was killed. She goes there every month with her mommy. I'm billing her for expenses, so we'd really only have to pay one fee. You and I can split it, and it'll be worth it for the manicure and massage. Go early Saturday, come back Sunday. I'm sure you don't have any Easter plans."

Lakshmi's Hindu family, of course, didn't celebrate Easter, and with my dad out of town and Shane working almost every weekend, there wasn't going to be much of an Easter egg hunt around my place, unless I hid the treats myself.

"I have to do an open house Sunday at two. Will we be back by then?"

"On Easter Sunday? You must be kidding."

"Nope. Talk about motivated sellers."

"We'll be back whenever you decide. We're going in your car, so it's up to you."

As embarrassing as this was to admit, I didn't know how to drive. A born-and-bred downtowner, I'd always found it faster, cheaper, and easier to walk, bike, or take public transit. My lack of mobility was often an issue in my band days; it was kind of hard to lug a set of drums around on the bus. Maybe that was why I'd usually stuck to just singing at gigs and rarely played drums.

"I should have known I'd get to be the chauffeur," Lindsey said.

"Listen, I have to get to work at the Smut Shop. I'll make reservations and email the Mapquest directions to you."

"How are we supposed to dress for something like this? I've never done a spa weekend before. Do I need to go shopping for something with Lycra? Or maybe hemp clothing, like those drawstring pants?"

# Wednesday, 10:15 p.m.

"So what are you wearing?"

"Black fishnets, a garter —"

"Cheerleaders don't wear fishnets." The masturbatory horndog on the other end of the line was paying more attention to my fantasy costume than I was.

"Sorry, Coach," I said. "I thought you'd like a naughty cheerleader."

"If you're not in the standard blue-and-white pleated skirt with matching pom-poms, you'll be benched."

And so it went on for another twenty-seven minutes. The cheerleader thing was so dull; about one in four callers requested this run-of-the-mill fantasy. However, this caller had pre-paid for a thirty-minute call, and it was up to me to give him an *O, R, G, gimme an A, S, M … what's it spell? Orgasm! Orgasm! Yeaaahhhh. Orgasm!* Kill me now.

I'd brought the photocopies from Rebecca's wallet with me. There were business cards from high-end restaurants and lounges, all in trendy, upscale neighbourhoods. Of course, there were the requisite business cards from hair salons and places where they spread melted beeswax on your legs and rip the little hairs from your body. Frequent-flyer memberships and preferred clients cards from Hertz, Air Canada, and a few other travel companies. But most of the cards I'd copied were from doctors, all general physicians, in various inner-city neighbourhoods, some of which were pretty dicey. Gee, add the myriad doctors to the collection of pills in her purse, and it was easy to figure out how she had such a variety of apothecary delights in her bag. None of this explained the sniffles, but if they were caused by allergies, then why hadn't the pill collection contained any antihistamines?

One business card stood out from all the others. With a brother and a cousin in finance and investments, why did she have a card from Terry Snider, a financial adviser with a Bahamas business address?

# Thursday, April 9, 9:45 a.m.

I love stupidity and naiveté, which described the way most people were when it came to privacy and security, especially online. Pouring a coffee, I sat at the kitchen table, phone in one hand, mug of java in the other. A few nuggets had teased at my brain when I got home from work last night. I was sure things were more obvious than I realized, but I had to step back to see the big picture. Ideas had been spinning around in my head when I went to bed last night, and it took a long while to shut down the grey matter and get to sleep.

However, this morning, the nebulous thoughts had morphed into concrete decisions about what to do and whom to talk to. I had a feeling today would prove to be very successful.

I called the first airline for which Rebecca had a frequent-flyer card. "Yeah, I just want to know my points balance."

"Just to let you know, you can access your frequent-flyer account via our website."

"I know, but my Internet server is down."

"No problem. Just for verification, what's your date of birth?"

I gave the date shown on Rebecca's driver's licence.

"And home address?"

Again, I thank thee, Ministry of Transportation.

"And last, may I have your mother's maiden name?"

Why did everybody use that as their security question?

"Oxford." Good thing I'd paid attention to Belham's thumbnail sketch of the Hanes family tree.

"Very good. Now how may I help you?"

"I'm not sure if my points balance is up-to-date. I think it should be higher. What are the last two trips you show?"

"You earned two thousand points for a Toronto-Freeport round trip March 8 and 9. Before that, also two thousand points for Toronto-Freeport, January 25 and 26."

"Okay, well, I guess that's correct then, so I don't need to send in my boarding pass as proof of travel?"

"No, you don't. It's current. Is there something else I may do for you today?"

"Yes, please. I want to check my seating for my next trip. Do I have an aisle or window?"

"You have the window seat out on Saturday. The return on Sunday, unfortunately, is quite crowded. You have the middle seat. I can get you an aisle seat if you take the 7:00 p.m. instead of the 1:00 p.m. Would you like me to change it?"

"No thanks. What time does the one o'clock flight get back?"

"You'll land in Toronto at 4:13 p.m. in Terminal One."

"I guess that's it then."

"Thank you for calling and enjoy your trip with us."

I didn't need an investigator's diploma to figure out that monthly one-night trips to the Bahamas could only mean she was playing "Hide the Illegal Funds in an Offshore Account."

Could this somehow relate to drugs? Maybe. Did it relate to the murder? Quite possibly. I had a strong feeling that the Bahamas thing more than likely had something to do with Rebecca's rat-faced brother Darren.

———————————————————

Mr. Belham's secretary put me through right away.

"I'm sorry to bother you again, sir, but I need some more help."

"Certainly. What is it?"

"It might be more complicated than a phone call. Do you have any time available to see me today?"

"Is the matter confidential?"

"Not really. I just need you to explain some things to me."

"I'm having lunch at the Blue Room with an associate at noon today. If you come at approximately one o'clock, we should be finished our business discussion. Join us then for a coffee."

"Perfect. Thank you."

The Blue Room was a much snazzier place than my usual haunts. What the hell could I possibly wear?

A waiter effortlessly set my coffee down in front of me and then disappeared. The staff in this place were exceptional, completely unobtrusive, yet they seemed to anticipate customers' wants and needs even before the clients did. The coffee was accompanied by a little silver tray holding a porcelain jug of cream and a silver sugar bowl.

I used little silver tongs to dump a couple sugar cubes into my coffee and then began talking with Belham.

"Well, sir, it's all really strange, and kind of suspicious." I filled Belham in on all that I'd learned in the past couple of days.

I leaned forward in my comfy teal wingback chair and took a sip of dark roast. I was wearing the most conservative clothes I owned, actually the only conservative outfit I owned, given my rocker chick wardrobe. The navy linen slacks and white silk blouse I had on was my standard job interview uniform, from back in the days of yore, whenever I had looked for a real job, which was rarely. I think I had always been destined to work for myself. Something about rules and office politics and playing well with others had never clicked for me.

I had accented my wannabe Bay Street attire with a slim gold chain and small gold hoop earrings, and looked suitable for the locale. My hair, blond and unruly at the best of times, was pinned up in what I hoped passed for a classic chignon. I crossed my fingers that it would stay put till we left the good ol' boys lounge. Belham's lunch companion had just left, and the old guy and I were lingering over our coffees.

Once upon a time, this brass-and-leather library-cum-dining-room would have had a humidor filled with the finest hand-rolled Cuban cigars, but the Smoking Police had put an end to that post-prandial indulgence. Too bad. Even though I didn't smoke cigarettes, I did enjoy the odd cigar, especially a Partagas. Must be a Freudian thing. I'd have to work cigars in to my next smutty cheerleader orgasm-on-call.

"I can't imagine any reason to do monthly overnight trips to the Bahamas aside from some funny money business," Mr. Belham said.

"The thing is that his sister Rebecca goes, not Darren."

"All the better if you're trying to maintain a few degrees of separation."

"Okay, I'm out of my league, so to speak. Finance isn't my thing. People are. Humour me. Hypothetically, what, how, why would someone be doing funny money stuff in the Bahamas?"

"The 'what' part is easy — money of dubious origins. I won't speculate what kinds of sources, suffice to say ill-gotten. 'How' and 'why' are easy and complicated at once. Bahamian banking laws are quite different from those of Canada or the United States. Essentially, the banks there ask very few questions. Most people,

I assume, are somewhat aware of the reputation and secrecy of Swiss banks. The situation in the Bahamas is quite similar, but without the transatlantic flight and shift in time zones."

"Interesting. Okay, next question. Did the dust-up with Darren and the Ontario Securities Commission a year or two ago have anything at all to do with insider trading or something along that line?"

I'd been mulling over the Darren-Investment angle, and the only thing I'd come up with was the Martha Stewart School of Stock Trading.

"I'm reluctant to comment on that, since nothing was ever done officially. However, yes, there were whispers along those lines."

Okay, well, Darren sure seemed to get out of it or get away with it or something. There was no way in hell he could spend afternoons in a pool hall picking fights with visible minorities and still play financial adviser to the well-heeled crowd.

## Thursday, 2:45 p.m.

"How about if I play the winner?" I asked, following custom and calling dibs on the next game by placing some coins on the edge of the pool table. "I'd love to play you." Darren gave me a head-to-toe once-over, and I was sure his mind's eye saw every curve beneath my outfit. *Ick!*

"Wish me luck," Darren said as he lined up for the break. His opponent this afternoon was a twenty-something skinny dude you could tell had never finished high school.

I'd missed lunch, so I bought a bag of vintage potato chips and sat on one of the chipped wooden bar stools, the varnish long since worn down to a dull finish by an endless series of denim-covered asses. I was feeling horribly overdressed and out of place, sipping my cola out of the can and watching their game. At least I was dry, but I bet I wouldn't be by the time I got home. The sunny spring weather had been shoved aside by some angry-looking clouds and, of course, I didn't have an umbrella. I'd smartly left it at home where my brolly could stay nice and dry.

Darren missed his next shot by a hair — a sneeze would have been enough to tip the ball off the precipice and into the pocket. The skinny dropout sank his next two balls and then missed what should have been an easy shot. Darren moved in for the kill and ran through the rest of the balls.

"Looks like it's you and me now, doll."

Did he lick his lips when he bestowed that slimy lupine smile upon me? Please tell me I imagined that.

"Terrific," I said, giving him one of my full-wattage smiles. Then I chalked up a cue and tried to look as if I'd done this before. I had no hope in hell of winning, but I figured a game together would be an incredible bonding experience.

"Ladies first. You can break. What are we playing for?" Darren had collected some bills from Dropout, but I was definitely not in this for the money.

"How about if we just play for a drink and some conversation afterward?"

"You're on."

I sank the number two on the break and missed my next shot. Darren wasted no time running the table yet again.

*Crack!* He sank the eight ball in the side pocket as promised. Thank God it was a quick game, because I truly didn't enjoy playing pool. Too much control and too much concentration for this ADD prototype.

"I guess you owe me a beer," Darren said. "Another game?"

"Mind if we just sit down and chat for a while?"

I bought us a couple of bottles of beer, and we sat at a table up front near the window, next to an out-of-order jukebox. Very little light came in through the window, which was more a comment on the weather than the cleanliness of the pane of glass, though I doubt it would have passed a white glove test.

"Your sister, Rebecca, told me I could find you here."

"Yeah, I noticed you here yesterday. What do you want?"

He seemed friendly, but I sensed a real edge to him, and I knew it was best to try to keep things light and fluffy. I'd rather he take me for an attractive academic than a journalist, because I was certain he'd clam up just to be ornery if he felt even slightly on the defensive.

"I'm a psychology student at the University of Toronto. I'm doing grad studies in psychology, with a focus on bereavement." I gave him the song and dance I'd given Rebecca. I guess I was the right skin colour and gender, because the Darren who spoke to me today was nothing like the jackass I'd seen here yesterday. "How about telling me a bit about Gordon first?" That seemed as good a way as any to get started.

"I don't know what to say. Gordon was my cousin, my only cousin. We're a pretty small family. We had a few years between us, but we were close, you know?"

I asked the kinds of "impact of bereavement in the aftermath of violent death" questions I thought a grad student would ask and got pretty much the answers I'd expected.

"Any ideas why someone would kill him?"

"Nope. Cops think it was just random, but I don't know. He wasn't carrying his wallet or any cash. The only valuable was his iPod, and that was still on him when the cops came."

"Do you believe it was something else then?"

"Some days I think so. I don't really know. If it wasn't random, then who? Why does this matter, anyway? I thought you wanted to know about the victim's family and stuff?"

"My thesis focuses on two groups of people, two kinds of murder cases, those whose killers were caught and are now in jail, and those that remain open. I'm contrasting the grieving processes." Holy fuck! Where did I come up with that?

Darren talked about Gordon for a while longer, and I listened with one ear and scribbled some notes I'd never read on a little notepad I'd dug out of my purse. Absolutely nothing he said was useful for my real intentions. We had finished our beers and were well into our next bottles, and Darren, while not obviously drunk or slurring, seemed more full of piss and vinegar now than when I arrived, enough so for him to put his hand on my knee. *Barf.* I was just starting to plan my exit strategy when fate intervened on my behalf.

"Hey, Darren, there's a call here for ya." The bored guy at the cash couldn't have picked a better time to interrupt us.

"Excuse me a moment, will you?" Darren said to me.

I stood and slung my purse over my shoulder. "Actually, I really must be going. I'll be in touch."

## Thursday, 4:10 p.m.

"**Y**ou haven't been in touch. I want to know what you've accomplished." How I wish I'd looked at call display before answering my cell. Christine's voice sounded about as melodious as nails on a chalkboard.

"I'd be more than happy to update you. Shall I email a progress report to you, or would you like me to fax it?"

"Neither. I'll be at your office in half an hour."

And if I had my way, I'd be on the other side of town when she showed up.

I took my time getting to my office, and Christine was wearing out the carpet in the hall outside. Pacing along behind her was a pair of legs dressed in pants so short they didn't cover the white sports socks that glaringly clashed with the black Gucci dress loafers they sprouted from. I couldn't see the face above the bad outfit, hidden as it was behind an ostentatious bouquet of red, pink, and white roses, but I knew without seeing the face that it was Victor.

"Hi, beautiful, I've been waiting all afternoon for you. This lovely lady's been keeping me company for the last while. She said if we put a bit of sugar in the water the flowers will last longer, so would you like me to trim them and arrange them for you?"

Victor, as usual, was speaking a mile a minute, and as usual, I really wished he were anywhere but in my presence.

Several months ago he'd come to me as a client. He'd suspected, rightly, that his wife was cheating on him. The pictures I had of her and an oh-so-unsexy bearded man were pretty damning. Victor cried like a baby when I gave him the news about his cheating wife. I consoled him ... imagine me hugging a grown-up nerd and handing him tissues while muttering soothing comments about how he deserved so much better, he'd meet someone else, she wasn't good enough for him, *blah blah blah*. Not my forte to play the sympathetic friend, especially since he was nothing more to me than a client. Victor had paid me well for my services, and as a bonus, had fallen hopelessly in love with me. I was so blessed … not.

"I'm sure you're very busy working on a case. Christine told me you're working for her, but if you have any free time at all I'd really like to take you to dinner, and even if we can't go out tonight, I still wanted to give you some nice fresh flowers because I was thinking of you and I have a gift for you, here, look."

He handed me an MP3 player. "I can't use it because I have this thing with my inner ear, and I get kind of wobbly and fall over when I listen to music up close like that because it makes me lose my sense of balance, you know? But I loaded all the songs on it that I knew you'd like."

I scrolled through the play list, and sure enough, all my favourites were there. Victor had included a range of hair-curling heavy metal, tried-and-true classic rock, gritty old blues, and a lot of peppy Broadway soundtracks.

"This is great, but you really shouldn't have," I said.

"Please don't thank me. I bought it and found out after that I can't use it, so I might as well let someone else enjoy it. Anyhow, about dinner, I was hoping —"

"*Whoa!* Easy there, tiger. The flowers are nice, and so is the MP3 player. Thank you. But dinner's not happening. I can't mix business with pleasure."

I was walking back and forth in my tiny office, trying not to trip over Christine, who looked bored and impatient. I was attempting to find a suitable vessel for the flowers. A jug of water I'd left on the radiator in an old-fashioned stab at a low-tech humidifier seemed to fit the bill.

"Well, I'm not a client anymore. It's been a while now, and Allison and I are divorced and it's all done and I'm ready to move on and —"

"Sorry, Victor. I don't think I can date you." And there wasn't a chance I ever would no matter what circumstances we'd met under. "But Christine here is single." Holy crap! That earned me a withering glare. Tough. "And I bet she'd enjoy a nice dinner and good conversation."

"What do you think, Miss …? I'll just call you Christine. Dinner would be nice. I know a place in Scarborough with all-you-can-eat ribs. It's really nice and casual, the kind of place where you can throw peanut shells onto the floor, so you don't feel all stuffy and uptight like which fork should I use, right? And they serve the best Bloody Marys in big old Mason jars, with a nice crunchy stick of celery, so we can go for dinner tonight if you want. They don't need reservations. I'm not even sure if they take them, but —"

"I have plans this evening. Perhaps another time. In the meanwhile, Ms. Jackson and I have business to discuss. If you'll excuse us …" Christine's clipped words should have snipped the balls right off Victor, but he was either too dense to notice or too desperate to care.

"I understand. You ladies have work to do and I won't keep you. Sasha can give you my number, Christine, and we can go out tomorrow or —"

"Let me check my schedule."

Victor backed up and out the door, his thumb and pinky extended next to his ear, mouthing the words "Call me."

"And don't worry, Victor," I called after him. "I can also give you Christine's number." Boy, could I ever. *Oops!* Another withering glare from Her Bitchiness.

"I trust you said that just to get him out of here," Christine said once Victor had closed the door behind him.

"Kind of. But now that I think of it, why don't you give him a chance? He's really smart and very sweet."

"What's he do? No, wait, never mind. He's definitely not my calibre. Does he have money?"

If it walks like a shallow bitch, and talks like a shallow bitch, then it probably is a shallow bitch.

"Lots. He's an inventor. He has a bunch of patents for a bunch of electronics stuff I'll never understand, and a few gizmos I'll never use. Mostly kitchen stuff, believe it or not. He's an engineer officially, but works for himself now, tinkering in his basement and getting lucky more often than is statistically probable."

"Hmm. I still don't think so."

"Probably just as well. I doubt he'd want to have a second woman take a big bite out of his net worth. The last one gouged him, even though she'd cheated on him. Nice guys finish last, as they say."

"Okay, now back to me," Christine said.

"You brought him up."

"I did not. Anyway, it doesn't matter. We're supposed

to be talking about my case, and what I hired you for."

I stuck my arm straight out in front of me, slightly raised, palm flat. "*Ja wohl! Ich wille, meine Kapitän!*"

"Very funny. Now tell me what you've been up to."

"Well, I saw Rebecca and Darren. They both think I'm doing graduate work in psychology and that I'm researching effects of bereavement."

"What did you think of pasty-faced little Becky? Quite the cool customer, isn't she? All doe-eyed and delicate, but trust me, she's no saint. I think she's a fake. There's a real undercurrent of volatility there. I mean, really, the angelic thing is just an act. She threw a drink in my face, don't forget."

"I know, I know. I had to talk to her, though. How else am I going to get a picture of what was happening in the life and times of Gordon Hanes if I can't learn about him from the people he's close to? Was close to, especially around the time he was killed."

"I guess. But don't believe a word she says. She'll probably backstab me, if she hasn't already, as if she doesn't have any flaws."

"Your name didn't come up, really. Remember, I said I'm a graduate-level psych student, so we talked mostly about his death and how it affected her. I also talked with Mrs. Hanes and Ted Chapman. Told them I'm a journalist writing a follow-up story on unsolved homicides."

"*Oooh*, Ted Chapman. Now there's a dishy guy. How I wish I'd hooked up with him before I met Gordon. There's no chance he'd ever date me now. It wouldn't be proper after being engaged to his best friend, but it's too bad. Ted would've been perfect for me, but some other girl is going to hit the jackpot with him."

*Mmmmm ... Ted. Teddy. Teddy Bear. Teddy Bare* ... "He's a catch? I hadn't really noticed." I had actually dreamed about him last night. It wasn't an X-rated dream, which was kind of disappointing, but I'd woken up with a warm fuzzy feeling, anyway. *Mmmm ... shoulders ...*

"And what about Maureen?" Christine asked. "Mrs. Hanes?"

"What can I say? A grieving mother. She seemed happy to talk about her son. Once she got started, she kept going. Told me all about his childhood, his favourite toys. The dog they had when he was younger. She sure seemed to like having an interested listener."

"Yeah, of course, she would. He was her whole life. So what's your next step?"

There was no way I wanted Christine to know that I still needed to reassure myself about her, so I didn't broadcast my plans for the spa, an idea I was already starting to regret because a little voice inside told me I'd have trouble getting paid anything at all, much less reimbursed for expenses, from Señorita Fashionista.

"I have a few threads I'm going to yank on. I don't want to get into details right now, though, okay?"

"I'd really prefer to be kept abreast of developments. After all, I *am* paying you for your time."

"True as that might be, it doesn't mean you get to tell me how to investigate."

"Pardon me?"

"You heard me. I work for myself. If you'd like to become an investigator yourself, I'd be happy to mentor you."

"I hardly think so." A pause. "Okay, how about if we reconnect after the weekend? I'll be visiting relatives in Muskoka, so perhaps I'll touch base on Monday."

"Monday's dicey. Most businesses are closed on Easter Monday, and everyone's closed tomorrow for Good Friday. I probably won't have much news to report by then."

"Fine. How about Tuesday?"

"Sure thing. Give me a call first, though. I have no idea yet how the day will unfold."

## *Friday, April 10, 10:30 p.m.*

Good Friday was a statutory holiday, and as much as nine-to-fivers appreciated the shortened work weeks, holiday weekends irritated me. Banks and government agencies — my two mainstays of investigating — were generally closed for days of observance, so I couldn't get any work done. Anyway, the days of the week rarely mattered to me. My investigating schedule was so flexible and sporadic that the day of the week hardly registered. *I'm off. I'm working. Eight days straight. Two weeks between clients. Three clients at once. I have no client and nothing to do. I've just worked twenty-six hours non-stop.* And so on.

The phone sex job was equally flexible. I usually did two nights early in the week and occasional weekends if I was broke or if they were short-staffed. One of my smut-talking co-workers had asked for tonight off, so I spent Good Friday talking about bondage to a guy with a Russian accent, then described an imagined threesome for an elderly-sounding man with a lisp. Maybe his dentures were loose.

There was a full moon tonight, and I swear it brought out all the kooks and crazies. Yes, in the world of phone sex, there were varying degrees of nut jobs.

After the old fart, there was a rare call from a woman who wanted to have phone sex with another woman. I didn't play for my own team, but hell, nothing else about the world of commercial phone sex was touched by reality, so why would I even think that orientation and sexual preferences would be? I moaned and groaned as she described in explicit detail everything she wanted to do to my body. At least she was a talker, so I played Solitaire on the computer while she described her fantasy. I won three games in a row, then switched to online job search boards. Maybe it was time for a change.

The next call was a crank caller, a giggly pubescent boy who had pilfered Mommy's credit card. He snickered every time he said the word *penis*.

I bookmarked a few help wanted ads for local fast-food joints. Maybe I could put my voice to good use on the drive-through intercom.

Good Friday. Good grief. By the end of the shift, I almost hoped someone would hang *me* up and stone me.

# Saturday, April 11, 9:15 a.m.

"We need for you both to empty your purses. It's our policy. Some clients try to sneak in no-no's like candy and chocolate bars," said the desk clerk at the Crystal Cove Spa.

Lindsey was getting pretty pissed off at the check-in procedure. "I have nothing to hide and nothing 'contraband,' but I still don't want anyone to go through my purse."

I had expected the strip-search greeting, and just for fun I'd filled my bag with a whole bunch of bubble gum, taffy, jellybeans, and what used to be penny candy but now cost upward of a dime per sugary morsel. They had confiscated all of it.

"For the next thirty hours, you'll purge your body of the toxins you get from poor eating habits." The scrawny clerk with her granite complexion and tombstone teeth was hardly a walking advertisement for the "New and Improved You" espoused by this holistic hell. Lindsey glared at the clerk once again and opened her bag. I was all smiles, enjoying Lindsey's obvious discomfort.

"I think this will be a great retreat," I said. "One question, though." I couldn't resist stirring up shit. "Where's the smoking section?"

The Wellness Nazi just about fell over at that one.

After we dumped our things in our room and changed into T-shirts and tights, we made our way down to the yoga centre. It wasn't just regular stretch, pose, and hold torture. No, no, no … that would be too easy. This was "hot yoga," with the room temperature set just degrees below that of the oven used by the witch in Hansel and Gretel. There were fifteen of us in the fifty-minute session, and everyone was pretending to enjoy sweating en masse. A cool shower and a cool glass of water followed the session, then it was off for my mud wrap (Golden Moor Mud no less!) and something called hot stone treatments. After that, Linds and I booked facials and pedicures. Lucky me, I was first up for the facial. Meanwhile Lindsey relaxed with a magazine on vegetarian cuisine and stuck her toes in a mini-Jacuzzi saturated with Epsom salts.

"Nice to meet you. My name's Willow. Have a seat right over here." Willow indicated a plushy reclining chair in front of a mirror dimly illuminated by a row of scented candles. "Just relax and get yourself comfortable. I'll start with the shitake mushrooms, then move on to orange rinds, followed by microdermabrasion."

"You're going to put mushrooms on my face?" I said. "You must be kidding."

Lindsey chirped in. "She's just being shy. Mushrooms are her favourite. Got any portobellos you can slap on her ass?" The aesthetician didn't look amused.

The treatment actually felt kind of relaxing, even though whatever the hell rejected salad fixings she smeared on my face smelled horrible. The scented pillars of beeswax did little to offset the pungent stink.

"We'll finish with aromatherapy and you'll forget about the odour of this stuff. I know it's not pleasant, but it gives the very best results. Trust me, your skin's going to glow and feel ten years younger."

"Knock yourself out. Sorry if I'm being difficult. It's just that I've never done this kind of thing before. It's all new to me. Actually, my friend recommended this place. Maybe you know her? Christine Arvisais?"

"I remember Christine, of course. She used to be a regular here, but we haven't seen her for several months."

"Has she been seeing another spa? Have you been cuckolded by a younger, sexier aesthetician who 'understands her'?"

Willow laughed. "No, nothing like that. It's just, well, I'm sure you know about her financial situation. We haven't really seen her since the money dried up."

"Of course."

What? Financial situation? The little voice that had had me on red alert the other day ... Damn, I hadn't checked yet to see if her cheque had cleared. *Play along, Sasha, play along.* People didn't mind gossiping about what they thought was already common knowledge.

"I guess that was insensitive of me. We're good friends and I know the money has been tight lately."

"I'll say it has. Her last cheque to the spa bounced. She was such a good client over the years that the management eventually wrote it off. Hers and her mother's bills." Willow was massaging pulverized peach pits on my forehead as she spoke. "I think the manager called it a 'valued guest promotion.' Anyhow, we haven't seen them since then. I guess they're embarrassed."

"Probably. Christine's very proud. Her mom is, too. So when did all this happen?"

"I guess it was sometime last summer. Why?"

"I'm thinking maybe I could treat her some weekend," I said. "I bet she misses coming here."

"I know she'd really like that. Unless she's too proud to accept a gift like that."

So where did Christine's money go? And how much could I sucker Willow into telling me before I crossed the lines of acceptable salon and spa gossip?

I nudged the chit-chat along. "It's hard when finances peter off the way they did for her family."

"I'd hardly say they petered off. If her mom didn't gamble so much, they'd probably still have a good cash flow. Mother and daughter used to make a detour to Blue Heron Casino on their way to or from their weekends here."

"You're right. Games of chance ... they've been the undoing of a lot of people." Oddly, and luckily, it wasn't that way for my dear old dad, and I didn't think such would ever be the case. Gambling was a science to him, not a sport.

"And lotto, and horses, and someone told me Mrs. Arvisais even goes to bingo. Can you picture her in a bingo parlour?"

I deepened my voice. "B-10, calling B-10. G-54, four corners, or fill out an X or a box and your card's a winner. O-70, calling O-70."

Willow laughed softly. "I shouldn't be making fun of her, but I can't see it. The horse races maybe, Monte Carlo or some high-end place in Atlantic City maybe, but not a bingo parlour with ladies wearing spongy pink curlers and track suits."

I let the conversation meander after that. It was obvious Willow couldn't tell me much more, but it was equally apparent that Christine wasn't the spoiled little rich girl she pretended to be. However, if money problems had been on the horizon, that would have been a motive to keep Gordon alive and work on a reconciliation with him and his Rosedale trust fund. Hmm.

The facial now complete, it was time for my pedicure and Lindsey's facial. After that we were off to our wellness class: What Colour Is Your Aura? *Dude, I hope it's tie-dyed.*

The next morning Lindsey and I were both cranky as we headed down to our imaginary breakfast.

"Yeah, yeah, yeah … sure my skin feels good, but I'm not a big fan of drinking potions and tonics to cleanse my system," Lindsey said.

"Me, neither. After all that organic wholesome roughage they gave us yesterday, this morning I could practically shit through the eye of a needle."

"Our first stop when we get the hell out of here is going to be a doughnut shop or burger joint, whichever we see first."

"I'm in. Two of whatever it is."

The seating arrangements for breakfast had us at tables of six. Our four carrot juice companions were all on the wrong side of middle-aged, and all so uptight that I could tell none of them had been laid in so long they now had tumbleweeds down there.

A teenage server pushing a tea caddy appeared at our table. "What would everyone like? I have just about every herbal tea imaginable."

"I'd like jasmine," one middle-aged lady said.

"I'll have a pot of peppermint if I may," her companion chirped.

The teenager served the two women, who were next to me, then turned to me.

"I'm looking for something in an un-oaked Chardonnay," I said. "Preferably something from the Pacific Northwest or Okanagan."

The woman next to Lindsey stifled a chuckle.

"Okanagan? You mean apple? Sure, I have two kinds of apple teas, one with cinnamon, one without."

"What vintage is the one with cinnamon?"

Lindsey rolled her eyes at me.

"It's fresh. I make all the teas to order."

Dingbat.

"How did the four of you become friends?" asked Lindsey, ever the gracious one in a new social milieu. One never knew who might eventually become a client.

"We were roommates at Queen's University," replied the roly-poly brunette at the head of the table. "We shared a house at 214 William Street, wonderfully close to campus, which would have been great if we'd actually attended classes."

The girls all chuckled at that. I could picture the wholesome, rosy-cheeked, pony-tailed, Icelandic sweater–togged group of them getting their education at what many considered a winter camp for the over-privileged.

"And did you shake your pompoms on the same cheerleading squad in high school?" I asked archly.

The cheekiness was lost on Roly-Poly, and she lapsed into nostalgic reminisces of the days when she still had her cherry and her natural hair colour.

I ignored the conversation for a while and sat silently wishing I had the morning newspaper — not to read it but to eat it. Breakfast consisted of tea, water, juice, and a few slivers of raw produce. My mind focused on what type of doughnut I'd get when we split this place. Maple or choclate? With cream filling or not?

"We sure had fun in those days. And we all married well."

"Maureen got the best catch."

My ears pricked up, and I let go of my sugar-glazed fantasy for a moment.

Roly-Poly continued. "All that Rosedale money."

"Not that she needed it. She was already so stinking rich."

"True. But she also got more respect and status after they wed. Marrying into the Hanes family did wonders for her social circle."

"Do you mean Maureen Hanes from Toronto?" I interjected. "Rosedale?"

"Yes, that's her," Roly-Poly said.

*Oh, boy, mother lode here I come!* Small world, but then not really surprising given that Christine came here with her mommy and that her mommy was an acquaintance of Gordon's mommy.

Roly-Poly, whose name was Frances, was a chatterbox, and needed little encouragement to gossip about the gals and the good old days.

"Over the years we've all been jealous of Maureen at times, and then have felt sorry for her at other times."

"What do you mean?" I asked.

"Well, she married very well, then was barren for many years. She had money and social standing, but never seemed to enjoy any of it."

"Yes, but it improved over time," said the woman on Lindsey's right.

"I guess so. Then she had her son, and you've never seen a happier mother. A few years ago her husband died, and she was back in her shell."

The severe-looking woman to Frances's right joined in. "She took such pride in Gordon. He was the only thing that got her through the death of her husband. Keep in mind, at this time Gordon was just coming into his own. He'd finished his degree, then started his career and got engaged. Maureen was on the upswing again, especially when the wedding plans were announced."

The gaggle of matrons all concurred.

"So what about now?" I played dumb, easy to do on a morning when I was deprived of my usual two mugs of caffeine.

"Well, again her world came crashing down," Frances said. "First Gordon broke off the engagement. A few months later he was killed when he was out jogging. A mugging gone wrong, I think."

"What a shame," I said. "Why did he break the engagement?"

"I'm not sure. My daughter knows some of Gordon's friends, and she heard some gossip, but nothing definite explained it."

"Maybe he just realized he was engaged to a bitch," I suggested.

An uncomfortable moment of silence passed. The severe-looking woman spoke next. "I'm unsure I'd call the fiancée a 'bitch,' but she certainly could be … abrupt."

"Who was she?" I felt as if I were holding the Best Picture envelope at the Oscars and that the small circle of Toronto's social elite was about to reveal all.

"Christine Arvisais was from a pretty good family, too, though they didn't have nearly as much money as the Hanes family. They have even less now. Her parents divorced a few years ago, and Christine's mother, Solange, hasn't yet remarried. I don't even think she's linked to anyone these days."

"Poor thing," interjected Frances. "In her world marriage is about the only option she has for a source of income."

"You know what they say — marry for money and you'll earn every penny," I said.

"Keep in mind, dear, Solange, like the rest of us here, is too old to go back to school. She's never really worked, save for putzing around at the art gallery and dabbling in charity events or fundraisers. If she ever had a real job, it would have been thirty years ago and would have been something entry level, you know, suited to a university student."

"What kind of education does she have?" I asked.

"Nothing that would help her these days. She did a fine arts degree, and years later bought the galleries, more for bragging rights than for profit. Her daughter runs the galleries now."

"I see. So what's the big deal about the money situation? I'd bet my last dollar she took her ex-husband to the cleaners."

"I've no doubt she made out quite nicely with her settlement. But half of what they had at the time of the divorce was all she got. No ongoing alimony these days. Christine's all grown up now, so no child support. Money keeps going out, but none is coming in."

"I see."

Shake the money tree and see what falls out. More often than not, money played a big role in whatever cases I was working on. Some say it's the root of all evil, but I say it's the root, trunk, branches, and all.

## Monday, April 13, 9:55 a.m.

I was standing in front of the bank a few minutes

before it opened. It wasn't as if Christine's cheque was all that stood between me and the line for food stamps. I mean, I lived with my dad (thirty-something and so proud!), I ate at Shane's place at least a couple of times a week, and I had a decent little stipend from my stint in the slut mines. I just hated feeling burned or ripped off, and what I hated even more was working for free. Unless I chose to do so, and that was certainly not the case this time around.

"I just want my bank book updated, please."

The teller, as studiously unfriendly as bank tellers are meant to be, silently took my book and shoved it into the printer. Her disapproving glare at the page before she returned it to me told me all I needed not to know.

"You're overdrawn. The cheque you deposited was returned NSF. Not sufficient funds."

"Yeah, yeah. I know what NSF means. Okay, then, let me transfer funds from my savings."

"Sign here, please."

"And I'd like to make a withdrawal."

"Sign here, as well." She wordlessly processed the transactions and then handed me five twenties. "Will that be all?"

"All I need now is a smile from you," I said in the most saccharine voice I could muster.

Her face nearly cracked as she reluctantly pushed the corners of her mouth upward. "Thank you for doing business with us and have a nice day."

I bet any other person would say her tone was even, but to me she sounded sarcastic and derisive, as if she took great pleasure in my getting stuck with a bounced cheque. The teller was probably just bitchy about working Easter Monday. Unlike the government, banks in Ontario only had a statutory holiday for Good Friday but were business as usual on Easter Monday. Too bad for my cranky teller.

Now what?

I was only a few blocks from Yorkville, so I decided to pop by Chadwick's and say hello to Becky. Lucky for me, retail establishments were also open on Easter Monday.

Unlucky for me, Rebecca wasn't in.

"She'll be in tomorrow. Did you have an appointment? I'm sure another one of our associates would be able to help you." The Heroin Chic Mannequin Cosmetics Chick flashed a smile that made me wish I'd never drunk red wine or black coffee.

"No appointment. It's more social than professional. I told her I'd drop by today if I was in the neighbourhood."

"Well, she was supposed to be here today but got delayed a day. She's out of town and missed her flight back yesterday."

"Right ... she did tell me she was going away. I guess a lot of people do the family thing on Easter weekend."

"She'll be on shift tomorrow. Would you like to leave her a note or something?"

"No. I expect I'll be around, so I can stop by and surprise her. Thanks."

Well, I had a surplus of time on my hands and no pressing engagements. My to-do list was malleable and

uninspiring, therefore easy to ignore. I was out and
about and wanted to stay that way, because I knew if
I went home, it would be too easy to let laziness and
frustration take over the rest of my day. I found an
Internet café and spent almost no time finding out that
Easter Monday was a bank holiday in the Bahamas.
I then used my cell to call the airline and once again
pretended to be Rebecca. Yup. I confirmed that "I" had
changed my return. No doubt Rebecca hadn't thought
of the bank's hours of operation when she booked this
most recent offshore laundering excursion.

Since I was online and in an anonymous milieu,
I pushed the boundaries of privacy and snooping
and logged on to Rebecca's online banking. All the
photocopies of her personal info were still stuck in
a pocket of my purse. Her PIN was her birth date.
Sometimes things were just too easy. I put on the MP3
player earphones and zoned out to Radiohead while
poking through her transaction history.

Debit card payments at various drugstores.
Airline charges for flights to the Bahamas. A rather
modest biweekly paycheque from Chadwick's. Online
bill payments for her cell phone. A thousand-dollar
withdrawal every month, usually a day or two before
her flights to Freeport. No hotel charges in Freeport or
anywhere else as far I could find. No food or dining
expenses in the Bahamas. More than seven hundred
dollars spent on shoes last month. Holy crap, I hoped
they were comfy. Pre-authorized monthly payments for
her car insurance and her gym membership.

Nothing too terribly exciting. If she was laundering money, then where was it? One thousand dollars wasn't enough to justify the monthly trips. In fact, the airfare ate up more than half of that. I scrolled a bit farther into her history. The monthly thousand-dollar transactions began in August — last summer.

So where did she eat and sleep when she headed to the tropics? And what was with the monthly G-note? And how did that relate to Gordon's death, if at all?

I closed the browser page, clicked onto "Internet Tools and Options," and deleted all the history and cookies. The most anyone could ever prove, if Rebecca knew her banking info had been violated, was that some hacker at this location had snooped through her files. Good luck proving the snooper was *moi*.

I left the cyber café and decided to take a long walk while my brain tried to make heads or tails of the life and death of Gordon Hanes. I tuned out the rest of the world while I roamed around downtown, listening to The Kinks, Sublime, Amy Winehouse and Thelonious Monk. Today was once again a bit warmer than the usual April temperatures, and I ambled for about an hour until the aimlessness in my walking and thinking started to make me feel restless. I bought a newspaper and wandered into the nearest Starbucks. I figured my edginess would be offset by a bucket of steamy hot, dark-roasted caffeinated something with whipped cream.

I hadn't looked at a newspaper in a few days, but the news was nothing new. Tax increases. A robbery at a convenience store very close to where I lived. A

fire in a warehouse in the west end. Global warming.
Another politician accused of fishy finances. Bad news,
unpleasant news, mediocre news, and more bad news.
Then something caught my attention:

> Police have no leads yet in the murder of a
> thirty-two-year-old man from Burlington
> who was killed early Saturday morning
> in the Toronto area's 27th homicide this
> year. Math teacher Jeffrey Keilor was
> shot in a parking lot near Lakeshore and
> Cawthra. His body, with two bullets in
> the head, was discovered at two in the
> morning by a security guard making his
> nightly rounds.
>
> Keilor had played his weekly
> basketball Friday evening with a group
> of friends. After the game, they had
> a snack and a "couple of drinks" at
> the usual local pub. The friends then
> headed off in separate directions. Two
> who lived in the area walked home,
> another hailed a cab in front of the pub,
> and Keilor, the only one who did not
> live in the area, went to retrieve his car
> just after midnight.
>
> Keilor was a high-school teacher
> and was very involved in after-school
> programs. "He was cool, you know?
> Like you could talk to him after

track meets, about anything. And I never liked math, but he helped me understand it, you know," said Warren Crandell, a grade eleven student at Swansea Collegiate.

Colleagues expressed grief and outrage. "This is senseless. He was so young. He was great with the students. He would have been a great dad. Now he'll never get to marry, have his own family. He would have made a difference. We'll really miss him," said Principal Annabelle Esterbrook.

Keilor was previously engaged to Angela Livingstone but ended the relationship a few months ago. "I still love him and we were working things out," said a distraught Livingstone. "He was the one for me. Now he's gone."

The murder story was sad, as stories like that always were. The accompanying photos showed the parking lot where he'd been found and an inset picture of the victim. He was borderline handsome, kind of boy-next-door-ish or generic, like one of those composite police artist sketches.

I lapsed into wondering about my latest client. Was it significant that Christine's family finances were kaput? What was the deal with Rebecca's trips to the Bahamas? What about her collection of pharmaceuticals? If none of the people close to Gordon had any idea why he was murdered, how the hell would I find out who had killed him? What was the real story with Darren? The link between him and his sister and funny stock trades seemed obvious, but what did it have to do with anything? And if the slime buckets were all so easy to spot, then what was I missing? I'd cottoned on to a couple of dirty secrets very easily ... what if Gordon had known bigger, more lethal secrets? Secrets people would go to any length to protect? And what about Ted? Could any guy that handsome and charming really be so flawless? And what should I look into next? The one thought that just wouldn't stay out of my head was that the aborted nuptials and the date of Gordon's murder were significant.

No answers were coming to me, so I went home. I was sure that putting things out of my head for a while would spawn a new train of thought by tomorrow.

At home I got back online and spent some quality time with my faithful servant, Google. I searched online for anything I could find about Christine, Darren, Rebecca, and even Mrs. Hanes. I came up with a lot of social notices, peer group and alumni stuff, and various puff pieces. Donations to the children's hospital, photos in the social pages of the Toronto media, some press releases about the galleries, mentions of graduating classes from university of this and prep school that. I found the business websites for Darren and Gordon's investment company, the corporate sites for Christine's galleries, and I even glanced at the online site for Chadwick's. I tried unsuccessfully to find any of the cast of characters on Facebook or MySpace. No dice. I looked up Paxil and the other pills in Rebecca's bag to learn more about them. I Googled bed-and-breakfast establishments in Freeport.

Three hours of surfing would have sated my voyeuristic tendencies if I'd had any, but other than that, it was a fruitless expenditure of my oh-so-precious time.

I changed into a pair of boxer shorts and an oversized T-shirt and locked myself in the music room I'd created in the basement. Headphones on, sticks in hand, and I was on my way to hard rock bliss. I smashed away at the drums for about two hours. My arms were sore by the end of it and my hands felt as if they wanted to self-combust. The journey into Head Banging La La Land decompressed me enough to spend the rest of the evening fused with the couch, my eyes glued to the TV.

The one thing I couldn't get out of my mind was the math teacher's murder. The mention of another cancelled engagement and another violent death gave me the heebie-jeebies. I had no idea what it could be, but I felt there had to be a connection.

# Tuesday, April 14, 10:20 a.m.

There was no reason for Rebecca to tell me every little detail of her life, but there was also no particular reason for her to lie to me. Either way, I decided to drop by Chadwick's and see what she said about her R and R over the long weekend.

"Nice to see you again." Rebecca was arranging a countertop display of glittery tubes and potions. Even the empty packages looked too costly for my budget.

"You, too, Rebecca. I was thinking about the cosmetics samples and the new lines you were getting the other day. I don't really wear much makeup, and, well, I was wondering if you could help me out with choosing a few things."

I was only sort of playing dumb. In the rocker chick days, I used to slather on a lot of heavy makeup well suited to the dark bars and stage lights. My prowess, or lack thereof, with liners and blush was of little consequence to frat boys tossing back jugs of lager. And in my day-to-day life I needed little more than mascara and a bit of lip gloss. Maybe *need* wasn't the right word: try couldn't be bothered spending energy on anything more than that.

"How about if we try some of these eye shadows on you?" Rebecca indicated a palette of earthy matte tones. "It's not busy right now. I can either show you how to do just your eyes, or we can spend a few minutes longer and do a full application. What do you think?"

I noticed she hadn't been sniffling and brushing her nose today, so I figured her hands were more or less germ-free. "Hey, if you have the time, I'd like to try a bit of everything."

For the next forty-five minutes she tickled my pores with soft brushes as she swept powders and potions across my face. I knew I'd wash it all off as soon as I got home, but for now the makeover bought me more than half an hour of her undivided attention.

"So, Rebecca, did you do anything special for Easter weekend?"

She hesitated for a moment before answering. "Just the usual. My family always drives to Kingston to spend it with my grandmother."

*Liar, liar, pants on fire.* "Nice to get away and spend some time with the family."

"Yes, it was lovely. What about yours, Sasha? Did you have a nice Easter?"

"Easter is usually pretty quiet around my house. We tend to do more family stuff in the summer."

"I see. Okay, now tilt your eyes up to look at the ceiling and don't blink." She held the wand of a sixty-five-dollar mascara and was about to lengthen and separate my lashes so they'd have a smudge-proof fullness for the rest of the day.

I tried to keep the idle conversation going. "I haven't really been out of town for a while. I think I might look into some last-minute vacations and see about going south for a few days."

"I'm sure you can find some good sell-offs at this time of year," she said.

"I hope so. I've kind of got my heart set on a beach somewhere sunny, maybe the Caribbean. Any suggestions?"

Technically, the seven-hundred-plus islands of the archipelago known as the Bahamas weren't part of the

Caribbean, but there was no point in quibbling over geographic trivialities, was there?

"Guadeloupe and Martinique are both really nice. I also like the Dutch Antilles, but I haven't been there for quite a while."

"I guess it comes down to what's affordable and what's cheap, as long as there's a nice beach. The only other thing I really care about is language. My Spanish is rusty, and my French sucks. I don't think I want to spend a week trying to figure out how to order food."

*Hint, hint, that's all the segue you need to mention Bahamas. C'mon now, I'm waiting. Any minute now.*

"We've often done sailing vacations around the islands," she said. "St. Vincent and the Grenadines are beautiful."

I had to feign interest now that I'd brought up the topic. So we chatted for a while about vacations and beaches, languages and airport hassles, salsa music and parasailing, but I gleaned exactly nothing useful about her quick little jaunt to Freeport. Why wouldn't she simply mention having been there?

"Now tell me what you think," Rebecca finally said.

She handed me a magnifying mirror so I could inspect her handiwork. I had to admit she'd done a great job. I was made up, but not tarted up, and my face felt better than it did after all the goop they'd slopped on me at the spa. Smelled a lot better, too. The colours she'd chosen suited me well and enhanced what Mother Nature had blessed me with. I felt guilty enough after the time and effort she'd spent on me to break out the plastic and buy a few things.

"Okay," Rebecca said. "It comes to $316.84."

*Holy fuck? How much? Threehundredandwhat?* For a mascara, eyeliner, two lipsticks, and some blush? How about my first-born child instead of my Visa?

"Here's my card." I said a silent prayer that my Visa wouldn't be declined.

The register spat out a copy of the bill. I signed the sales receipt in blood and wondered about the store's return policy if the cosmetic packages remained unopened.

"And here's your free gift with purchase." Rebecca handed me some tanning lotion with SPF 75 and aloe vera. Okay, that made it all worthwhile.

An hour or so later I was in my office thinking what a waste it was to be all made up and sitting alone in a barren office. I checked my email and decided I didn't want to claim my prize from the Nigerian National Lottery, nor did I wish to enlarge my penis, since I didn't have one and hadn't even seen one in a while, at least not since Mick and I had broken up. I also didn't want to sponsor the immigration of my long-lost cousin from Malaysia.

The only thing worth reading was a nice but brief email from Dad. He was into his third day of playing blackjack at Turning Stone Resort and Casino on the Oneida Indian Reservation in Upstate New York, not far from Albany. His email talked about the success of his latest card-counting theory, which had so far earned him twenty-two hundred dollars, after expenses for food and lodging. I sent an email reply, asking if I'd now finally get that pony I'd always wanted.

My voice mail was equally uninspiring: two messages from Victor asking for Christine's phone number, an automated telephone ad from a moving and storage company, and a very terse message from Christine. Apparently, I had just missed her call. She had told my machine she'd be in my office within the hour, no later than three o'clock. It was now ten after two, and I wondered if I could duck out before she —

"Now listen up and listen good. I did *not* hire you to investigate me. What the hell were you doing asking around about me? Do you have any idea how embarrassing this is? You're fired."

Guess it was too late to sneak out the back door. Today Christine looked even more like a bitch than before. Her little black suit was a perfect complement for her black soul, and the red blouse underneath it brought out the red in her eyes. I couldn't help but think of Cruella De Ville and wondered if I could find a purse-sized Dalmatian to accessorize her ensemble.

She placed both hands flat on my desk and continued yelling at me. "People from the spa have been talking. Old friends of my mother have called. Everyone wants to know who my nosey 'friend' is. Everyone's commenting on my mother's finances. People are wondering about her low profile. Rumours are flying from the masseuse to the yoga instructor to the clients and back again. You have a big fucking mouth, and I've never, ever been happier to terminate a business relationship."

Throughout her whole tirade my eyes never left the computer monitor on my desk. I filled in square after square in the daily online crossword. Four across: a Jewish festival, five letters, beginning with *p*. If the puzzle asked for a nine-letter word for bitch, the answer was standing right in front of me.

"Okay."

"Okay? Okay? That's all you have to say for yourself? Okay? I should report you to the Better Business Bureau. You've been completely unprofessional, you've ruined my reputation, and you've acted totally irresponsibly. I hope you get your licence revoked. In fact, I'll see to it that you do."

"Okay."

"And not only that, but I'll be putting a stop payment on my cheque for your shoddy, incompetent, fraudulent services."

"Okay."

Was she in complete denial, or did she really have no idea her cheque had bounced? And if she were that clueless about money managing, then what did that say about the financial viability of her art galleries?

I gave her my very best expressionless look. "If you have nothing more to add, then please leave. You said yourself that I'm fired, so you're no longer my client, and as such, you're now trespassing. Get the fuck out of my office."

I guess Christine had pretty much run out of steam by that point. She picked up her designer purse, turned on the heel of her designer shoe, and marched out of the office without bothering to close the door behind her. I think the purse and shoes were both knock-offs.

Why hadn't I mentioned the bounced cheque to her? There was no point in doing so now. The money wouldn't have magically appeared and the mention of the bounced cheque would only have made her more venomous and the confrontation more volatile.

The whole exchange made me mad, but it also made me more … curious? More resolved? More stubborn? I hardly thought that was possible. More something. I had free time now that my only (ahem) paying (ahem) client had turfed me. No other contracts were waiting in the wings. I wasn't on shift at the smut shop till later in the week, and my interest had been piqued enough to want to get the real story about Christine. If she hadn't fucked with me, I could easily have forgotten the whole thing. But she had made it personal. I'd been fired by better people than her and by people with better reasons to fire me. And I'd never been fired by someone who had stiffed me on the bill. Of course, none of that was on my company website.

# Tuesday, 6:55 p.m.

"**I** think Shane's trying to kill us," I said.

Lindsey and I were having dinner at Shane's restaurant.

"Maybe he's just trying to make me fat so he can keep all the other guys away from me," Lindsey said.

We were feeling no pain — full bellies, empty heads, an explosion of tastes in our mouths, a couple of very dry gin martinis with extra olives before dinner, a bottle of wine with our meals, and now we were pounding back ice wine with our white chocolate parfaits. Talk about getting our "just desserts." It was good to indulge.

"How about a couple of Spanish coffees after this?" Lindsey suggested.

"Sure, but lean in front of me for a minute. I have to undo the button of my jeans."

"So Christine had the nerve to fire you?"

"Yup."

"Even though she never paid you?" Lindsey asked.

"Yup."

"What are you going to do?"

"Well, for one thing, you're getting stuck with tonight's bill."

"That doesn't surprise me. Good thing I'm sleeping with the chef."

"Why do you think I'm your friend? I know he's my brother, but even I wouldn't take advantage like this."

"Nice. So I guess you'll never get to the bottom of the Case of the Fatal Former Fiancée."

"I'm not sure what I'll do. She signed an agreement with me and I did provide the service. She just didn't like the method."

"You could take her to small claims court and try to get the money she stiffed you out of."

"Maybe. I need to think it over for a day or two. Plus there are a few questions I still want to answer, client or not."

"Like what?"

"Motives, money, matrimony, murder. The usual."

"You should follow the news stories about the guy who got killed last weekend. Maybe that case has some parallels that'll help you solve everything."

"Weird coincidence, eh?" I said. "The papers quoted his ex-fiancée. She said she was hoping to reconcile. But that's about the only similarity, really. The guy last weekend moved in a different social circle, high-school teacher, strictly middle class. Didn't even live in Toronto. Hamilton or some sub-sub-suburb."

"Burlington."

"Right. Anyway, with the math teacher guy, it was late at night in an isolated parking lot, not broad daylight in an open area. I don't think the Burlington guy and Gordon have anything in common except for both calling off the wedding."

"And both being dead."

# Wednesday, April 15, 11:29 a.m.

"Good morning. May I please speak with Sasha?" I didn't recognize the male voice, but my brain recognized the throbbing pulse of four hundred chimpanzees break-dancing in my head.

"*Ugmpuhg.*" My throat was parched, and it felt as if I needed to shave my teeth. "This is Sasha. Who's calling?"

"It's Ted Chapman. Is this a bad time?"

The digital clock by my bed said eleven-thirty in the morning. I thought eleven-thirty at night would still be too soon to interact intelligently with anyone other than a four-year-old. How many Spanish coffees had Lindsey and I drunk last night? And what the hell else had we consumed? After dinner we'd hit the Horseshoe Tavern for our quota of live music. The country-rock band had been pretty good, but the crowd was dull. So we'd wandered west for some Gothic ambience and possibly a few shots of Jaegermeister. Sometime after that we'd ended up in a karaoke bar on Spadina Avenue.

I recalled singing a rap version of a couple of Dolly Parton songs while Lindsey tried to do backup vocals. God, what a mess! I was sure it would have deflated Dolly's boobs if she'd heard it. I barely remembered the cab ride home, but at least I was fairly certain I hadn't puked in the taxi. And it was comforting to see that I'd awakened fully clothed and in my own bed.

"No, it's fine." Note to self: Sexy man on the phone, so try not to sound like an idiot. "What's up?"

"I think we need to talk. I just got off the phone with Christine."

Oh-oh.

"She told me everything. How she met you, that you were working for her, and that you're not a journalist."

Oh-oh.

"I'm not a psychology grad student, either," I admitted.

"What?"

"Never mind. I guess the cat's out of the bag. Sorry for being duplicitous." It sounded more like I'd said *dooplithitoosh*. Why hadn't I just chosen an easy-to-pronounce, two-dollar word like *sneaky* instead? "But it goes with my job."

"I called Christine to see if she'd talk to you about your article on grieving. She filled me in and tore a strip off you in the process."

"Sorry. I'm sure you're mad about it. It's just one of the things I have to do when I'm working on a case."

"Well, I don't know if *mad* is the right word, but it's moot. I think it was a good idea for her to hire you."

"You do know that she fired me yesterday?" I kind of felt like a loser admitting this to a guy who seemed to have it all together. *Teddy Bear, Teddy Bare …*

"Yes, and if you're available —" *ooohh, yes, I'm available, but for much more than you intend* "— I want to retain your services. Keep looking into this. Someone has to, and the police never got anywhere before, and aren't likely giving it much effort now. Dig around, see what you find."

"Sure. Sounds good."

Working for Ted equalled good. Working for Ted equalled being near a living, breathing example of masculine perfection. Working for Ted equalled how the hell would I concentrate? Working for Ted equalled I bet *his* cheque wouldn't bounce. Working for Ted equalled oh, shit, my head hurt and I couldn't think of work until someone removed the colony of army ants parading through my veins. Working for Ted equalled maybe I could break the rule about never sleeping with a client. *Shhh ... don't tell Victor.*

"Great," Ted said. "How about if I come by your office in a little while? After lunch? Say one o'clock?"

I gave him the address and made a beeline for the shower. Twenty minutes of scalding hot water followed by five minutes of absolute zero almost made me feel like a homo erectus ... Speaking of erect, I flashed back to Ted's broad hands and thick fingers. Make that ten minutes of ice water, yikes!

Twenty minutes later, lathered, lotioned, and blow-dried, I put on my MP3 earphones to smother reality. Today's song selection was a mixture of jazz piano tunes, just the thing to drown out the cruel, cruel world. I walked up to Danforth Avenue and hopped onto a subway train, wonderfully oblivious.

# Wednesday, 1:09 p.m.

"Okay, you know the story I told you. What else do you know?" I was as put together as was possible, given the residual self-inflicted damage from last night's bender. Ted, on the other hand, looked as if he'd walked off the cover of *GQ*.

"That's pretty much it. Darren and Rebecca don't know yet who you really are, unless Christine told them. My guess is that she probably will, if she hasn't already. Christine and Rebecca didn't get on well, but Christine and Darren are pretty tight."

"I don't want any of this to upset Mrs. Hanes," I said. "She's a nice woman, and I feel kind of bad for deceiving her." I took another sip of the takeout coffee I'd picked up en route and was embarrassed that I had nothing to offer Ted. My no-frills office didn't have the mini-fridge or mini-bar that the hardboiled dicks in all my favourite detective novels seemed to have. I was also embarrassed by my very obviously shaking hands.

"Don't worry about that," Ted said. "I'll talk to Mrs. Hanes. I think she'd support a private investigation. She'll never have peace until we get some answers."

"Okay. I need answers, too, if I ever hope to figure out what the heck's going on. You can help, but don't ask how I learned certain things, okay?"

"Certainly."

"This is all more hypothesis and suggestion rather than fact. Maybe you can fill in some of the blanks." Was that redundant? I really needed more sleep and a couple of Tylenols.

"Fire away."

"One: Rebecca Blackmore seems to like pills. Vicodin, Percocet, and some other high-octane prescriptions."

"She was in a car accident four or five years ago. She's had some back problems ever since."

"Do you know if she takes any other medications?"

"I don't think so, but I'm not really that close to her. I knew her through Gordon, and of course spent time with her over the years often. But she and I never had much in common. Since Gordon died, I've only seen her once or twice, generally by accident through mutual acquaintances. It's nice to catch up now and then, but we're not so close we'd ever call each other and meet for dinner or anything."

"Okay, what about her brother, Darren? He's as tightly wound as Rebecca is mellow. What's he all about?"

"I've never been a fan of his. I play the game when I see him socially, and occasionally professionally, but he's a hothead."

"As in violent? As in could he have had something to do with Gordon's death?"

"I don't think so, but you never know. See, the thing is that Darren is from a good family, he has money and the right connections, but two things keep holding him back."

"Oh, God, what?"

"First of all, there's the drinking. He's fine when he's not into the sauce, but he can really lose it if he has too much. Obnoxious. Belligerent. He'll start fights in bars, but always with some stranger over some imagined slight, and always with someone smaller than he is."

"Didn't strike me as the type who'd pick on someone his own size."

"Right."

"And the other thing holding him back?" At least I could come up with the obvious questions needed to steer this conversation. My mental acuity was on par with a soup spoon, and the best I could hope to accomplish for now was to receive and store data, but screw the possibility of processing any of it.

"Well, he's rather obtuse. Gordon was the brains behind the company. Darren ran the operation solo at first, but his father was helping him in the background. Gordon was still in university at the time."

"Keep going."

"So Darren had help and did okay, breaking even for the most part, but not really making much money for his clients. When Gordon came onboard, they really started to do well."

"Could Darren have been jealous?"

"Possibly, but probably not. Gordon and he shared all the portfolios. And Darren, believe it or not, can be quite charming. He was the one who schmoozed the clients. As long as he doesn't go overboard with drink, he can be very … gregarious. A lot of their client roster came from him. He's good at networking, so he was sort of the face of things. Gordon is … was … quieter, more serious when it came to work, so he stayed behind the scenes most of the time. Basically, Gordon was worth more to him alive than dead."

"Well, that's putting it bluntly. What about Christine? Where did all her money go? You knew when we spoke last week that Christine has champagne tastes on a beer budget."

"Yes, I did. Sorry, I had no idea at the time who you were and what you were doing, so it didn't seem appropriate to mention her family's economic situation."

"Fair enough," I said, "but we have a new set of rules now. So what happened to the family coin?"

"She never really had much in her own right. There was family money from her father's side while her folks were together, but they divorced a few years ago. She hasn't spoken to her father since they split up, hence bye-bye trust fund. Christine and her mother like to live very well, as they always have, but there's no income to match the outgo. It's like both mother and daughter are waiting and hoping to marry money."

"If they do, they'll work very hard to earn every penny." I recycled the old saw I had used at the spa.

Ted grinned and nodded in agreement.

"And their art galleries?" I asked.

"Her mom started them, at least the first one. I'm not sure about the one at Harbourfront. I think it initially seemed like a good fit for Mrs. Arvisais, you know, prestige in a way, a respectable job for someone in her circle, more of a way to see and be seen than as a source of revenue."

"I heard that gambling is part of the story. Her mother."

"Could be. Mrs. Arvisais is always the last to leave a charity casino."

"I heard she's into bingo and horses, too." That sounded like a kinky fetish request from one of my phone sex clients. I shivered.

"They used to co-own a couple of Thoroughbreds, but I don't think they do now. At any rate, gambling could explain a lot."

"Christine's cheque to me bounced."

"Was that before or after she fired you?"

"Before."

"And she still had the gall to dismiss you? What did you say to her?"

"I didn't even mention it. So where does this leave us?"

"I can give you cash if you're worried about *my* cheque." He smiled as he said this, and the sparkle in his green eyes briefly made me forget about my hangover.

A moment later a metaphoric sledgehammer upside the head brought the hangover back to the front and centre of my fragile brain. Victor, sans flowers this time, but still dressed in the worst of 1980s bargain-bin rejects, poked his head into my office. I was way too wobbly to articulate the thought, but once again I wondered how the hell he always knew just when to show up. My office hours were anything but regular, yet he always seemed to know when to find me here.

"Hello, Sasha, I see you're with a client, but I was wondering if we could go for a coffee after. I'm going to ask Christine out and I'm nervous. Maybe you can help me think of what to say. I'm hoping to take her for a nice dinner this —"

"This isn't a good time, Victor." His surprise appearance jolted me out of Sparkly Green Eyes Ted Land and into Nerds on the Prowl Territory.

"I know you're busy, so I won't stay, but can we make an appointment, maybe in an hour or two? Is that enough time? I don't know what you're working on, so maybe you need longer. I'm free all day, so I can wait around for you. I really want to take Christine out for a date. She's so beautiful, but I'm a bit shy and —"

"Victor met Christine when they both happened to be here a few days ago," I explained to Ted.

"You mean Christine Arvisais?" Ted asked.

Victor's eyes lit up at the chance to blather on about the object of his unrequited affections. "Yes, do you know her? She's such a beautiful woman, and I think I have a good chance with her. I just don't have a way to reach her, but I think if we went out we'd have a great time, and I think we have lots in common and I want to get her number from Sasha —"

"I have all her contact info," Ted said. "Here, write this down."

I bit my tongue to keep from laughing and handed Victor a pen and paper. Ted scrolled through his BlackBerry and gave Victor Christine's cell and work numbers, as well as the names and addresses of the two galleries. I kind of wondered why he had all her contact info so handy but figured that it was probably a leftover from her days as his best friend's fiancée. And they probably still merged in some of the same elite circles.

"Just FYI, Victor," I said. "Christine's no longer my client."

"Oh, did you solve her case already? You work so fast. I remember when you did my file and got such good results for me so quickly." He turned to Ted. "If you're thinking of hiring Sasha, I can highly recommend her. She's the best, and you won't be disappointed. I had —"

Ted jumped in. "That's good to know. Sasha will be taking care of a query for me. Now if we could get back to business?"

I seconded the motion. "Sorry, Victor, but this is confidential."

"I understand and I —"

Ted cut him off before he got started on another of his long-winded spiels. "You should surprise Christine with a visit at the gallery."

And with that, we simultaneously got rid of my annoying but passive geeky stalker and set the wheels in motion for Victor to become someone else's nuisance.

"Okay, back to Darren," I said. "I heard there was a minor kerfuffle a while back, about maybe doing some questionable stock trades?"

"Hmm, that. Well, you didn't hear this from me. Gordon was the one who rattled the cages at the Ontario Securities Commission. He talked to me about it before he called them."

"I need details." I jotted some notes on the computer while he spoke. My head was far too sieve-like to try to remember anything this potentially important.

"Well, like I said, Darren didn't really do all that well until Gordon came along. He just doesn't have the knack for it."

"And?"

"Then Darren got lucky. He bought a lot of stock that shot right up a few days later."

"Markets are funny sometimes."

"Then he hit another money-maker and then another. Gordon suspected Darren had the inside scoop."

"I can see where this is going."

"Exactly. Gordon asked Darren about the trades, and Darren shrugged it off. Remember, I didn't know any of this at the time. Gordon told me about it later."

"Keep going."

"So Darren claimed everything was on the up-and-up. Gordon took him at his word and thought that was the end of it."

"And, of course, it wasn't."

"Darren made another savvy purchase or two. And he sold off a couple stocks just before they tanked. It just didn't sit well with Gordie. He talked to me about it one night after work."

"What did he say?"

"His worry was that if Darren was doing something unethical, that Gordon would be tarred by the same brush, too, as they say."

"That's how it would look."

"So we talked about it for a while. I mean, this had been going on for several months. Not on a regular basis, exactly, just out of nowhere this guy started picking winners and selling losers just in the nick of time. It didn't fit with his track record. So Gordon made an anonymous call to the Ontario Securities Commission."

"That would certainly be a motive."

"True, if it fit with the timing. Remember, this all happened about a year before Gordie was killed."

"Hmm."

"And remember, Gordon was good at the markets. He was very smart. I can't see that Darren would kill him, goose that laid the golden egg and all, if you'll forgive another cliché."

"Any chance Darren knew that Gordon called the OSC?"

"I doubt it. When the OSC investigated, it looked at both partners. It was an anonymous call from a phone booth, and in the end nothing came of it. It was so long ago, so long before the murder, that I really don't think it connects."

"All right," I said. "I'll get started looking into other things. I have a few ideas. Will you let Rebecca, Darren, and Mrs. Hanes know I'm now working for you? They won't be much help if I can't get them to talk to me."

"Sure, no problem."

"I guess you'll need to tell Christine, too."

"I'm not looking forward to that call."

"Can we meet in a couple of days for an update?" On a day when I wasn't hung over. On a day when my brain was working at more than two miles an hour. On a day when I wasn't feeling like death warmed over. On a day when I put on something sexy.

After Ted left, I went down to the corner and bought another large coffee and a newspaper. My head was spinning, and not just from the hangover. I had more than enough threads to yank on and no idea which one to pull first. For some reason I kept thinking back to last night's salute to decadence with Lindsey. Something she had said really stuck in my craw, but I didn't know what and I didn't know why.

# Wednesday, 2:40 p.m.

I didn't usually look at the obituaries, but for some reason today I did. The funeral notice for Jeffrey Keilor jumped out at me as soon as I opened the "Health and Lifestyle" section of the newspaper. It occurred to me that this was an odd section in which to house death notices. I read the details for Jeffrey's service, then dug my cell out of my purse and called Lindsey.

"The devil got me last night," I said. "How are you doing?" As I asked the question, I knew what her answer would be.

"About the same. I'm never drinking again. Ever. My head still feels like it's made of glass."

"Well, since we both feel like the walking dead, want to go to a funeral with me?"

"Whose funeral? Mine? I really hope so."

"Death would be such sweet release. Jeffrey Keilor's, you know the guy from Burlington who was murdered. The service is tomorrow. I need a drive. Burlington's too far by public transit. Actually, I'm just too lazy.

And I truly doubt this hangover from hell will be gone by then."

"*Amiga*, you have to learn to drive. What time's it at?"

"Ten o'clock. And thanks. I keep thinking about what you said about him and Gordon both being dead fiancés. It's probably a waste of time, but I'm curious."

"I hope my blood alcohol is within legal limits for driving by tomorrow. I'll pick you up about nine."

Okay, so I now had a plan to do something, even if the something was of dubious value.

Rebecca, Darren, Bahamas, pills, pool halls — what did it all mean and did any of it matter? Christine would merit further digging, too, but not today. I hoped Victor was doing his pathetic little puppy routine with her. I hated to have fun at his expense, but Christine was such a bitch that saddling her with a lovelorn nerd was irresistible. I thought of strolling over to Chadwick's to see Rebecca, but I figured her serenely spacey self would be too much work for my slow-motion self. We'd likely both sit there staring silently at our coffees and muttering disconnected monosyllables. That left Darren and a long walk to the pool hall. It was almost three o'clock, and it was at least a forty-minute walk. I was still far too shaky even to think of hoofing it. *Yo! Taxi!*

Darren happened to glance up from the billiard table as soon as I walked in. He had just taken a shot and excused himself from his opponent. He moseyed, yes, really moseyed, over to the counter where I had just ordered a can of Coke, my third in less than a week, way above my usual intake. This one was medicinal, though. The sugar-and-caffeine buzz might help to bring me back to life.

"I'm almost finished my game. We need to fucking talk." His voice was gruff and his breath had that sour, beery stink that won't go away even with a few swigs of Listerine. "Don't fucking leave."

"Don't tell me what to do." Of course, I wanted to talk to him. Why the hell else was I there? But his cocky attitude brought out my inner bitch.

"We've got unfinished business," Darren said.

"Indeed we do. I'll wait for you outside."

"Don't fucking take off on me."

"Don't worry. I won't." I tried to sound confident and tough, but I doubt I pulled it off.

He nodded silently and returned to his game. I had no idea what the hell I was trying to prove in that little pissing contest. Making him come outside to me seemed like I had won a minor contest of wills, but it proved little since it was chilly and there was no bench or any place to sit while I waited. Boy, did I show him ... not.

About ten minutes later he joined me on the sidewalk. "I'm parked in the garage down the block. We can talk in my car."

For a fleeting moment I contemplated the wisdom of being alone with him in an enclosed, isolated space. In much the same way you could see your breath when it was really cold outside, I could almost see the hostility and potential volatility emanating from his pores. However, I had no desire to let him know that he intimidated me, so I followed.

No matter how questionable his source of income might be, he certainly enjoyed the benefits of living in a tax bracket, whether declared income or not, far beyond my reach. His ride was a fully loaded ice-blue Jaguar XK coupe in mint condition and with that new car smell. I think the car cost far more than I could get from the sale of both my kidneys.

"Christine fucking called me this morning and fucking told me who you are and that she fucking fired you."

"You said *fucking* three times in one sentence. Try for more variety in your vocabulary. It'll impress the chicks."

"Jesus Christ, woman, are you fucking asking for trouble?'

"Nope and I'm also not asking to spend a second longer with you than I have to."

"So why don't you fuck off?"

"You wrapped up your game, left the pool hall, walked a block down here with me, all so you could tell me to fuck off? Does it sound better to use the F word in a Jag or something? You fucking could have fucking told me to fuck off back at the fucking pool hall, you dumb fuck. See I can use the word, too, and much more creatively than you."

Darren glared at me, then committed what I considered an unpardonable act of vandalism or desecration or something. He lit a cigar, a big fat stogie, inside his beautiful car. I loved a good Cuban, but this was clearly the wrong place, wrong time. Bye-bye, nice new car smell.

"This isn't your business." He rolled down the window an inch or two and exhaled.

"Don't you care about what happened to Gordon? Wouldn't you like to see the killer in jail?"

"Yes, but I don't think a little girl like you is going to find anything the police couldn't."

"*Little girl?* Nice. Are you single? I can't imagine why no one's scooped you up yet. Charming and eloquent — there must be a lineup beating down your door."

"Spare me the sarcasm. You fucking know what I mean."

"Anyway, I'm working for Ted Chapman now, so this *is* my business, and it's his dime. So you can either talk to me or not, but either way I'll still be around asking questions."

"Ted? Jesus Christ. That wanker probably just hired you to get into your pants."

"That's it exactly. Lord knows he wouldn't choose me for brains and ability." I paused and waited to see who would break the silence. He kept drawing on his stogie and glowering at me. I gave in before he did. "This is ridiculous. We can sit here verbally sparring and trading sarcastic remarks, or we can sit in stony volatile silence, or we can talk about Gordon, your dead cousin. Your call."

"What do you want me to say? He's dead. He won't be undead. Someone fucking killed him. I have no idea who. Next?"

"How about why? There's always a motive. Money, revenge, jealousy, something."

"If I didn't know her so well, I'd think it was Christine. On paper she seems the most likely candidate. But she wouldn't have, couldn't have."

"What about a client? Something work-related? He must have lost money on some portfolios. An ex-girlfriend? A lover's triangle? A secret he shouldn't have known?"

"Nothing. On the romantic front, you know all you need to about him and Christine. They were engaged, then fucking broke up. Work? He was the golden boy. He made money for our clients consistently. Even his few bad picks were more than offset by gains elsewhere."

"Did he have any enemies? Any skeletons in his closet?"

"How the fuck would I know about skeletons? Enemies? None that I know of. My sister was closer to him socially. Ask her."

"How's your business doing now? If Gordon was so good, you must be in a pinch without him to steer things."

He chomped down on the cigar for a moment before answering. The stench of the stogie made my hung-over stomach churn. "What the fuck? I know what I'm doing. For Christ's sake, woman, I've been trading longer than he ever did."

"Could he have ever done anything unethical? Insider trading, funny transactions?"

"You watch too much TV. Our — my — company has an excellent reputation." He flicked some cigar ash out the window.

"Then why did the OSC snoop around once upon a time?" Hint, hint ... this would be a good time to drift into funny-money land.

"Oh, fuck, that? Just routine checking. I think some rumours got out of hand. They looked into things, saw it was all above board, and then they fucked off, which is what you should do. Get out."

Touchy, touchy. I wanted to slam the car door just to make a point, but it didn't seem right to vent my frustration on such a fine example of mechanical engineering brilliance.

My mood sucked. The weather had turned even chillier and more unpleasant. I shrugged deeper into my jean jacket and wished I'd put on a scarf or something around my neck. Then again, maybe the brisk air would force my hangover into cryonic suspension. The self-inflicted headache from last night wouldn't go away. I hopped into a streetcar and went straight home. There was no point in trying to salvage the day. I had a long, hot, sudsy bath and then went right to bed. I slept undisturbed for the next fourteen hours.

# *Thursday, April 16, 9:52 a.m.*

As if scripted for a low-budget Hollywood movie, the morning of the funeral was rainy and grey. April showers brought May flowers — who gave a crap? I'd just found out the hard way that my boots had a leak. Damn!

Lindsey glanced at me. "I hate going to funerals, even if it's not for someone I know. Knew. Whatever. They give me the creeps."

"Well, duh, I don't think anyone enjoys them."

"I bet there'll be a big turnout for this guy."

"Wonder how many will be voyeurs like us?"

The service was being held in an older Catholic church in the area people would consider the downtown of Burlington, if Burlington actually had a downtown to speak of. Lindsey and I had had to park a few blocks away, since it was even more crowded at the church than we'd expected.

It was easy to pick out the grieving family from among the throng of mourners. The family stood together, a quartet of red-eyed, black-togged people who probably enjoyed family Scrabble nights, but instead were here, prematurely burying a well-loved son and brother. The mother looked as if she baked homemade pies. Dad no doubt worked with his hands. The two sisters, both likely younger than Jeffrey, got their brown curly hair and dimples from their mother. A red-haired woman who didn't resemble the others was possibly the old girlfriend/fiancée. Like the others, she was dressed in black and crying, but she wept silently, dabbing her eyes with an obviously soggy tissue.

There were so many people in attendance that the family couldn't have known everyone on sight. After the service, Lindsey and I did the ritual *"I'm sorry for your loss, he was such a good person, what a shame"* condolence thing, then went to the basement for free coffee. We helped ourselves to Styrofoam cups of watered-down, rancid brown liquid and powdered cream substitute and then stationed ourselves within earshot of the several pockets of muted conversations near the table of gratis cookies and squares.

"The poor family ..."

"His father is taking things so stoically ..."

"Jeffrey was so young ..."

"It's such a tragedy ..."

"Poor Angela. You know, she hadn't told anyone yet, but she and Jeff had worked things out and were going to get married, after all ..."

The last comment came from a small huddle of thirty-something women. It got my attention.

"Linds, I gotta check out what they're saying. Stick around the goody table and see if you can get a line on the relatives."

"So, am I Watson to your Holmes? Cagney to your Lacey? Who was Nancy Drew's sidekick? Or could we get Jessica to join us and pretend we're Charlie's Angels? I've always wanted to be Jill. Farrah Fawcett was so cool."

"Ha. You're so funny. You should give up real estate and do stand-up comedy full-time. You'll have an HBO special in no time."

"Stick in the mud," Lindsey said. "Should I take notes?"

"Just listen and zero in on whatever seems odd or interesting or really gossipy."

I refilled my coffee cup and nudged my way closer to the trio of hens. "It's such a shame," I said to a woman who needed to spend some time on a Stairmaster. "They would've had a happy life together."

"So you knew, too?" Stairmaster asked. "I think it's an open secret. Everyone knows they were meant for each other. I think the stress and expense of the original wedding plans freaked them out."

"That's why their idea of a quick, private ceremony in Niagara Falls made so much sense," said another thirtyish woman, this one in a wrinkled suit.

I piped in again as if I belonged. "I remember Angela telling me they'd decided on this, but when were they going to do it?" I lied with the casual ease of one who spoke the truth.

"Near the end of May, whenever the long weekend is," said Stairmaster. "Quiet, no frills, no fuss. That's what Jeffrey wanted. He hated being the centre of attention."

"Yeah, all that stuff before about colour schemes, seating arrangements, and flowers," added Wrinkled Suit. "I think the wedding planner was what scared them. Angela called her the Nuptial Nazi."

"Right, she did mention that the planner was, um, very detail-oriented," I said. Yup, that's me ... just one of the girls.

"To say the least," said Wrinkled Suit.

"When I got married," said a brunette who hadn't spoken yet, "we didn't use a planner and I wish we had.

Our wedding almost led to divorce."

The girls all found that funny and tittered nervously.

The conversation lapsed into memories of weddings they had attended and bridesmaid's dresses they had worn, all pastel and puffed sleeves and tulle. *Yuck!* I muttered a few fictional phrases about my own organza extravaganzas, then excused myself.

Lindsey was communing with a group of teens who were obviously Jeffrey's students. They stood in tight little clusters, arms around one another or holding hands. No doubt for some this was a first experience with death. Almost every one of them had teary eyes, the boys as well as the girls.

"You can honour his memory by doing something in track and field," Lindsey said to them. "Maybe the Jeffrey Marathon, the Keilor Track Meet, or an athletic scholarship. Something to remember him by."

"Pardon me, Lindsey, can I have a word?" I asked.

"Sure." She hugged a couple of kids before we left.

"Let's go this way," I said, steering her out of the building and toward her car. Opening my umbrella, I tried unsuccessfully to cover both of our heads.

"That really wasn't so bad," she told me.

"Hear anything useful?"

"Not really. Most of the people I spoke to were from his school. Sounds like Mr. Keilor was very well liked."

"Apparently, the wedding was back on, but they were being hush-hush about it," I said.

"Really? Poor what's her name, the bride to be or not to be."

"Angela's her name. I wish I'd had a chance to talk to her, but there were too many people around."

"Do you have any way of getting in touch with her?"

"I'll think of something, but I'll wait a few days."

"Okay, so where am I dropping you off?" Lindsey asked. "What's on your agenda for the afternoon?"

"I don't know what I'll do. If you're pressed for time, you can just drop me at the GO Train station." The commuter service between the exurbs and Toronto was actually pretty fast and was almost always sometimes usually now and then once in a while reliable, kind of.

Lindsey shook her head. "No, no. I'm heading back to Toronto, just not downtown. I have to see a client in Bloor West Village. Can I drop you at Runnymede subway station?"

"Perfect. And thanks for playing chauffeur. I owe you one."

———————————————

If Lindsey's least favourite thing to do was to attend funerals, mine was being stuck in a subway tunnel. The subway train stalled between stations, just after Yonge Street. Nothing freaked me out more than being locked in a giant metal tube in a dark transit catacomb.

I tried to control my breathing. *Calm, stay calm. It's okay. There's enough air. We'll be moving in a moment.* I clenched and unclenched my hands. They were coldly sweating, and I dug my nails into my palms so hard I thought I'd draw blood. *Get me the hell out of here!*

A muffled voice came over the intercom. "Attention, subway passengers, we are experiencing a delay eastbound on the Bloor-Danforth line at Sherbourne station. Service will resume shortly."

I dug out my MP3 player and cranked it up as loud as I could stand. *Don't think about suffocating. There's enough air. Take a deep breath.* The rhyming optimism of Broadway soundtracks momentarily distracted me. Then, a second later, I opened my eyes, noticed my surroundings, and started to hyperventilate. *Mind over matter. We'll be moving shortly. Clench, unclench, clench, unclench, repeat. Another deep breath.* The train jerked to service about ten very long minutes later, and I bolted out the doors as soon as we pulled into Sherbourne, the next station.

Sherbourne was a few stops before Pape, which was where I usually got off to go home, so I had now spontaneously altered my plan for the afternoon. Since I didn't really have a clue what I was doing, it mattered little. I was within walking distance of either Mrs. Hanes's house or Yorkville and Rebecca. It was still raining, so I decided to try Mrs. Hanes first, since she was closer. I thought it prudent to call first.

No answer, not even an answering machine. Enter Plan B. I opened the umbrella and began walking west toward Chadwick's, my leaky boots making squishy sounds along the way.

# Thursday, 2:40 p.m.

"Rebecca? We need to talk."

Rebecca was showing one of her associates how to properly dust translucent powder on her forehead. I bet the makeup brush she used cost more than my black linen funeral suit. She shooed away her colleague and answered me without making eye contact. "I don't think I have anything to say to you. Darren told me who you really are."

"Did he tell you I'm now working for Ted?"

"It doesn't matter. You were sneaky, and I have no respect for anyone who'd exploit a situation for their own ends."

"My own ends? Excuse me, but I think my objective is in line with yours, isn't it? To find out who killed Gordon?"

"Look, this isn't the time or the place. I'm working and I have an appointment coming in soon."

"Fine, can we meet afterward?" I asked.

"What would be the point?"

"Freeport, Vicodin, Percocet —"

"What?"

"Bahamas, Paxil —"

"Enough. How about four o'clock at the roof bar in the Park Hyatt Hotel?"

"I'll be there."

I had over an hour to kill and wandered west in the rain to Avenue Road. I decided to browse in the new addition to the Royal Ontario Museum. The asymmetrical glass-and-metal architectural aberration that exploded from the classic old stone building was truly an eyesore. The expanded facility provided some great photo ops of old meeting new, but to me it looked as if the bowels of the old building had regurgitated a crystal mess. I could only guess what the inside would look like. I was standing at the corner, waiting for the light to change, when I heard my name being called.

"Sasha, hey, Sasha!"

Victor, soaking wet, was waving to me from up the street. How the hell did he always know where to find me? He held on to the waistband of his pants as he ran toward me.

"Hey, fancy meeting you here, Sasha." He ducked under my umbrella with me. "It's always so nice to see you, and it's good you brought an umbrella. I forgot mine at home. So where are you going on this day for ducks?"

"Just running some errands." I figured if I said the museum, I'd have an unwelcome escort.

"I was visiting Christine at her gallery. I don't think I'll pursue her, after all. She's very rude. I was there yesterday, and she rushed out to meet with an artist, so I told her I'd be back today and brought her a nice box of truffles. When I got there, I was going to ask if she had dinner plans and —"

"She gave you a very unsubtle brush-off, didn't she?"

"She wouldn't even accept the chocolates, so I gave them to a bag lady on the street. Imagine, not even the decency to accept a gift politely. At the very least —"

"Don't waste another second thinking about her."

"Well, it seemed like there might be potential."

Based on what? I wondered. "Victor, listen up and listen well. She doesn't deserve you. The right woman is out there for you, but you have to be patient. Don't come on too strong."

"Perhaps you're right. I'm just really eager to share my life with someone, and I want to start a family. I know I'd be a good husband and father. I have so much to give and only need someone to give it to."

This had all the marks of a maudlin monologue in the making. Time to curtail. "Listen, I don't want you to feel like *I'm* brushing you off, but the truth is, I'm working a case right now, not doing errands, and I need to concentrate."

"I get it," Victor said. "Maybe we can go for a coffee or a movie when your case wraps —"

"I'll let you know. This one might last a few weeks. I don't want to blow my cover, so I'd better get moving." Before Victor could say anything more, I hopscotched through a red light and ran into the ROM for an hour of mindless walking.

# Thursday, 5:35 p.m.

"What have you got for Pinot Grigio?" Rebecca asked as she joined me at the corner table on the penthouse level of the Park Hyatt.

The stuffy old waiter rattled off a few names.

"I'll have the Palmina Alisos," Rebecca said. "It's one of my favourites."

"I'll have the same," I said.

The waiter nodded and turned away.

Our seat didn't take advantage of the normally fantastic view of downtown Toronto and Lake Ontario, but on a wet spring day there wasn't much to look at, anyway. Besides, I didn't want other patrons to be within earshot of what was sure to be a testy discussion, so that also ruled out sitting at the bar, my usual preference.

"So what was that all about back at the store? Bahamas and Percocet? You seem to have a vivid imagination. Maybe next you'll claim I'm a secret agent or a member of the witness protection program."

"Rebecca, don't insult my intelligence and don't waste my time. What do you want to talk about first? Pills or the islands?"

"What do you mean pills? I don't take anything without a prescription."

"You have a pharmacopoeia cornucopia." I'd been saving that phrase for just the right moment.

"I have a bad back."

"Bullshit. Even if you do, that's no reason for OxyContin, Vicodin, *and* Percocet. And Paxil? That's not for pain. It's an anti-depressant."

"Okay, so I'm depressed. I don't think it concerns you."

"If you need help, you can get help, whether for pill addiction or depression or whatever. But if you're into forged scripts or dealing or something, you can get into a lot of trouble. So could your shady doctors. Who'd write the prescriptions for you if your doctors were reported to the medical association? Think any of them would risk a career for you?"

"If that's all you have to discuss, then this conversation is over." She took a big gulp of the wine the waiter had silently deposited on our table.

"You shouldn't mix pills and alcohol."

"I'll keep that in mind."

"What about the Bahamas?"

"What about it?"

"We talked about beaches and vacations, and you forgot to mention Freeport."

"It's not worth mentioning. I was only there for a short visit. I don't know it well enough to recommend it as a vacation destination."

"You go there every month."

"Have you been spying on me or something? Where the heck do you get your information?"

She hadn't raised her voice, but she was clearly rattled and on the defensive.

"Cut the crap. What's with the island junkets? And who's Terry Snider?"

And with that question I got the same surprise Christine had received last week at Monsoon — a glass of chilled Pinot Grigio in my face and an angry Rebecca storming out in a huff. The waiter appeared instantaneously, a stack of paper cocktail napkins in hand. I dabbed my eyes and smudged my mascara into a raccoon-like mask. Fuck it, I was unlikely to pick up any guys in this posh tourist hotspot, so it mattered little what I looked like. I stayed a while longer and finished my wine. At nineteen dollars a glass I wasn't going to waste it and was almost tempted to wring the damp napkins into my mouth.

Well, Becky sure had some stuff she wanted kept to herself, but her attitude made me want to dig and dig. I was halfway convinced — for no reason other than gut instinct and Rebecca's reactions — that the pills were a non-starter, but Bahamas and Terry Snider were worth a closer look. Wine in the face and uncontrolled emotional displays could only mean whatever she was hiding was sensitive. Time for me to start bulldozing into her private life. But what could I learn that I hadn't already?

I signalled the waiter for the bill. The wine-in-the-face rumpus embarrassed me into leaving an overly large tip. The waiter gave me a thumbs-up when I walked out.

Back on street level, the rain had stopped, but the sky was low and dull. Rush hour was just getting underway, and I had no desire to put my phobic self into a crowded train with weary nine-to-fivers. I hopped into the first taxi heading my way. The driver, who of course didn't speak much English, asked me three times for the name of my street. He obviously didn't know Toronto very well, since he kept plugging the misspelling of my street name into his GPS device and was getting an "item not found" message every time. I was a bit cranky — wine in the face and squishy boots will do that to a gal — and I preferred him to have his eyes on the road rather than on the electronic thingamajig. I barked directions at him, and ten minutes later I was in Riverdale. Home sweet home.

# Thursday, 6:20 p.m.

Back home I started climbing the walls, not literally but almost. I had the house to myself tonight. Shane was staying over at Lindsey's again, and Dad was still off on his gambling jamboree. Normally, I relished a quiet evening at home, but tonight I was skittish and needed a sounding board.

I tried to lose myself in music, hoping that drumming for a while would empty my brain. It had the opposite effect, though. Every song I played reminded me, in one way or another, of Gordon and the whole clusterfuck. I played some Ted Nugent and thought of Ted Chapman. I tried Guns N' Roses' "I Used to Love, but I Had to Kill Her" and pictured Gordon dedicating it to Christine. Nine Inch Nails' "Head Like a Hole" conjured up Jeffrey.

I put the sticks down and plopped in front of the TV. Even the most mindless sitcom seemed to hint at murder. A reality show featuring a bunch of washed-up celebs smacked of pill addiction. *Survivor* made me think of the

Bahamas. The Discovery Channel was showing mating rituals among zebras and, well, that suggested sex and reminded me that I'd been single too long.

I started thinking of Mick, my ex-boyfriend, and wondered if we'd called it quits too soon. In my heart of hearts I knew I still loved him, and I also knew we just weren't good together. We were both a bit hot-tempered and we were both stubborn beyond belief. But we understood each other and we had so much in common, so much chemistry.

Strangely, Mick and I had never wanted the same thing at the same time. When I was ready to give up on music, he was more committed to it. When I wanted to take our relationship to the next level, he'd gotten skittish. When I decided to walk away from him, he'd begged me to come back, promising me the sun and moon and stars, but I knew it would never last. In the time since the breakup, I'd met some very sexy guys, like Ted Chapman, and some really interesting guys, especially while I was at college. But none had had the magical combination of chemistry and being *sympatico* in every way, except in the big picture.

I gave up trying not to think, grabbed a pen and paper, and decided to give in to my overly active grey matter. I wrote down, in my hieroglyphic script, all the questions I wanted answered about the Gordon Hanes murder.

I'd irritated Darren easily. Why? I had also easily ticked off Rebecca. Again why? They supposedly cared for their cousin yet had no desire to help me find his killer. That could only mean they were involved in his death or had unrelated secrets they didn't want me to stumble across while I investigated. But what? Why had Christine been so quick to fire me? Why had Ted been so quick to hire me?

I needed someone to help me see the great big bushy green forest in front of my eyes, so I paged my father. I would never, ever, say this to his face, but he always knew the answers before I even asked the questions, and he'd helped me figure things out much more often than I'd ever admit.

When he was at the tables, it was hard to draw him away, so I knew better than to sit by the phone, willing it to ring. I went into the kitchen and nuked a bag of popcorn. Then I sat at the table and played about eight or nine games of Solitaire while I waited for Dad to call. I lost every game and was about to nuke another bag of Orville Redenbacher's finest when the phone clanged to life.

"Hey, Dad, how's the trip going?"

"Oh, you know, up and down. Lost a few dollars today, but no big deal. Sometimes it's good to have a few losing streaks. It keeps the casino staff from making you as a card counter."

"Well, if they ever figure you for a professional player, you could always go in disguise."

"I might look good with a beard."

"And you could dye your hair or get a Mohawk."

We chuckled over that and then chatted about the mundane stuff of day-to-day life: Shane, the weather, the mail. Dad had been away for over a month and the pile of letters and bills was pretty thick.

"Just leave it for now. I'll be home in about a week."

"Okay. Listen, Dad, I need to borrow your brain. I have a case where I'm hitting nothing but brick walls."

"Shoot. What's it about?"

I told him everything I knew and all I surmised about Gordon and the circle of bluebloods to whom he was related. I mentioned all the peripherals, including Belham, the funeral in Burlington, lah-di-dah art galleries, the Ontario Securities Commission, and the gossipy women at the Crystal Cove spa, and even Victor's aborted courtship of Christine.

"So, oh, Wise One, what do you think?" I asked.

"Are you asking me for advice? Counsel from dumb old Dad? The day has finally come when you seek my guidance?"

"Stick it in your ear. You can gloat later, but right now I've got to make some kind of sense out of all this."

"Three things. Find out more about Ted. Why is he stepping up to the plate when the family won't? What did you say he does for a living?"

"I'm not sure. I never got around to asking him."

"Second, talk to the mother — what was her name?"

"Mrs. Hanes. Maureen Hanes."

"Right, talk to her again. Be upfront with her about everything. She probably knows more than she realizes, but she's too close to things to be objective."

"Okay."

"See if there's a connection between Gordon and the math teacher — what's his name?"

"Jeffrey."

"Right. See if there were other similar murders."

"Okay, got it."

"And four —"

"Dad, you said there were only three things."

"Senior's moment. I'm allowed to be forgetful at my age."

"Bet that serves you really well in card counting."

"I raised a smartass. Anyhow, four, find out what's bugging Darren. Something doesn't sit right about him. Rebecca, too, but I'd worry about the brother first. Sounds to me like she's nothing more than a bit player or a pawn."

"Once again, oh, Wise One, you offer brilliant advice, advice I might actually follow for once."

"I should've been stricter when you were growing up. Maybe then you'd respect your elders." He hung up.

Respect for my elders — yes, must work on that. Respect for the law ... well, I was usually pretty law-abiding. But tonight I was ready to really bend it. It wasn't a break-in if someone let you in, right?

---

Dad was correct. An idea had come to me after my conversation with him. It was time to find out more about Darren. The scheme I came up with might well be in the top ten dumbest things I'd ever done, but if it worked out, the payoff was more than worth the risk. At least that was what I told myself.

I dressed in a very sexy camisole and black leather

miniskirt. I put on pair of satiny sheer black stockings, with seams up the back. I shoved my feet into a torturous pair of black shoes with heels so high it felt as if I were breathing thinner air up there. I went into the dining room and grabbed three bottles of wine, one for show and two to hold in reserve as potential bribes. From the bathroom I grabbed a bottle of lilac-scented body lotion. From my bedroom I snatched two vanilla-scented pedestal candles. I hadn't had a date in months, but I sure had all the trimmings for a romantic soirce.

I maintained a degree of modesty by donning my beige London Fog raincoat over my outfit, and instantly felt like a flasher. The slutty shoes and hosiery still showed beneath the overcoat. However, the teasing suggestions they offered might later prove beneficial. On the way out I stopped in the den and grabbed a couple of blank computer CDs and a USB flash drive. A girl's gotta be prepared. I didn't bother with any condoms, though.

And off I went. I walked three blocks and was propositioned twice before I hailed a cab. At least the rain had stopped.

# *Thursday, 10:49 p.m.*

"Look, please, you've got to let me into suite 1103. My boyfriend will be so disappointed if I screw up this night."

"Sorry, Meees ... I cannot let joo in witout de key."
The janitor was a Latino male, about fifty years old,
and I wish I'd had a bottle of tequila to offer as a bribe
instead of wine.

"I understand. And I'd never try to get someone in
trouble. But, well, this is kind of embarrassing, but my
boyfriend has a fantasy and we planned to act it out
tonight."

*El janitoro* looked me over from head to toe. I
could read his mind and knew he was thinking unclean
thoughts. *Yuck!* I knew I could play him the same
way I played all the phone sex creeps at my other job.
Details. Give him details and he'd be putty in my hand
for as long as it took him to find an empty bathroom
stall and jerk off.

"Oh, jes? What is jor fantasy?"

"Well, I'm going to pretend to be the secretary and
he's going to get me to file some papers, then I'll drop
them ... and well, you know ..."

"How come joo no have the key if iss your boyfriend's office?"

"I do have the key. I just forgot it at home on the
kitchen table. I had to bring all this other stuff, and the
key slipped my mind."

"I no s'posed to open doors for no one. All the
tenants has a key."

"Let me give you something for the inconvenience."
I handed him the two extra bottles of wine and fifty
dollars. Without another word he called for the elevator.

We rode up to the eleventh floor in silence, though I could easily hear what he was thinking. He opened the door to Darren's office suite. "Maybe after joor boyfriend, joo wanna spend some time with me …?"

"I don't think so. My boyfriend's pretty jealous. Anyhow, he'll be here in about half an hour. I need time to set the mood. If he gets here early, don't ruin the surprise."

"I don't know nothin', *señorita*."

When the janitor left me alone in the suite, I put my purse and the bag of goodies on the floor by the door. I didn't have much time. The receptionist's desk, generic IKEA teak, was covered with small plants: a couple of cacti, spindly spider plants spreading off in all directions, a couple of other leafy things I didn't recognize, and a wilted African violet. A fax machine and a photocopier were to the left of the desk. Smack dab in the centre of the desk was a computer with a twenty-one-inch flat screen and a wireless mouse and keyboard.

There were two club chairs in the waiting area opposite the desk and some nice paintings hanging above them. The pictures were typical Canadian wilderness scenes, but the colours were more spectacular than the usual browns and greens. The painting on the left included various shades of mauve and magenta brightening a rural sky at dusk. I had to remind myself that I wasn't here to gawk at pretty artwork.

The side table between the two chairs had the usual array of current magazines: *Forbes*, *Time*, *Newsweek*, *Fortune*, *The Economist*, *The New Yorker*, and *Toronto*

*Life*. All were addressed to "DG Investments," and even I could figure out from whence came the company moniker.

I knew my area of interest was Darren's inner sanctum. I peeked through the window panel of one of the inner office doors and brilliantly deduced that his office was the one that looked as if it had some life in it. The other office, with the door ajar, was cold and empty except for the most basic furnishings and had obviously been Gordon's. It didn't appear that anyone had dusted in there for a while. I was careful not to touch anything.

Back at Darren's office door, it took less than a minute to pick the lock, and then I barrelled right on in. His sleek desk, his top-of-the-line computer, and his walnut veneer filing cabinets all promised to reveal a trove of goodies, but where to begin?

The desk drawers didn't merit more than a quick glance: paper clips, a bottle of Pepto-Bismol, pens, elastics, a pile of loose change, a pint of whiskey, and not much else. A bottle of gel-coated Aspirin, with one capsule left in it, rattled around in the back of the middle drawer. At least Darren didn't seem to share his sister's fondness for pills.

I wasn't a computer whiz, so I was under-enthusiastic about trying to glean anything from the computer on Darren's desk. I turned it on and waited a moment for it to warm up. No surprise — it was password-protected and I wasn't about to waste time playing guessing games. Instinct told me he'd be smarter than his sister about PIN codes. I had a paranoid feeling that unsuccessful attempts to access his machine would lead it to self-destruct or that alarms and sirens would begin blaring.

So I was going to rely on Theory A and Plan B. I shut the computer back down and eyed the two fake mahogany filing cabinets. They were locked, but that was nothing careful manipulation and a nail file couldn't get past.

The top drawer had a bunch of client files, all sorted alphabetically. I glanced quickly through the surnames but didn't recognize any. Abbott, Brown, Carmichael, Casson, Claremont, Durand ... Ground, Hansford, Harris, Holgate, Irwin, Lismer, Morrisseau ... Oxford, Ruiz, Taylor, Thomson, Varley ... Wilson-Young, and who cares who else?

The second file drawer had receipts and expense reports: phone bills, electricity bills, payroll records. The payroll log listed all of one employee, a receptionist named Wendy Cross, who earned fourteen dollars per hour sitting at the desk out front. I held on to the Wendy file — bit players often proved to be hugely helpful in my line of work.

The bottom drawer of the filing cabinet was the motherlode, but I almost didn't recognize it. There were corporate prospectuses, company profiles, and miscellaneous fact sheets for a number of companies in which Darren bought stock for his clients. Aquila Resources, Baytex Energy, Glamis Gold, Harbourfront Corporation, Hazelton Holdings, Marcus and Associates, Rio Can Estates — wait a second, back up!

Hazelton and Harbourfront. Christine's galleries. What the hell?

I took the two *H* files to the front area and photocopied everything in them. Minutes later they were back in their manila folders, looking just as they had earlier. Then I sifted through the Wendy Cross Receptionist file and saw all the usual payroll information: address, phone number, social insurance number, date of birth. Theory A was what I'd applied to pry into Rebecca's life. People were naive and chose the same old passwords they wouldn't forget. I flipped through her file and nosed around her desk. I turned on her computer, rightly expecting that for fourteen dollars an hour she probably wasn't paid enough to care a whole lot about corporate confidentiality. QWERTY wasn't it. Strike two for her birth date as her PIN. Third time was a charm. Sure enough, her phone number was the password. Dingbat.

I saw folder icons on the start-up screen labelled "First Quarter," "Second Quarter," and so on. There were a number of Excel files and a few Word documents. I stuck my USB flash drive into the appropriate port in the PC and copied as many files as I could. One spreadsheet was titled "Arv Transactions"; I suspected it would be the gold mine of them all. Arvisias, Christine.

Twenty minutes later the machine was off, the Wendy file was back in the cabinet, sheaves of paper were tucked into my bag, and the scented candles hadn't been lit. I was giddy as the elevator smoothly coasted to the lobby. My Latino janitor pal was half-heartedly cleaning the glass doors at the main entrance and seemed surprised at my early descent.

"Whas happening, *señorita*? Joo get stood up?"

"No, no, no. Nothing like that. My boyfriend called my cell and said he's been in a small accident. Just a fender bender. We're going to have to reschedule the fantasy night. I'll be sure to bring my key next time."

"Well, if joo has some extra time, we can —"

"Gee, you know, I'd love to, but my boyfriend needs me right now. I have to go pick him up. Here, have another bottle of wine for being so kind to me." I shoved the bottle into his hands and made a beeline out of there.

I was so eager to nose through the files that when I got home I didn't even change out of my slut attire, other than kicking off the death-defying heels. Curling up on the couch, I read through all the paper copies. Money in, money out. Painting sold. Money loaned. Money invested. Loan repaid. Painting bought. Commission fees. Interest. None of it really made sense to me, but I wasn't so dumb that I couldn't figure out that Christine was hiding money through Darren and/or he was laundering money through her galleries.

I cranked up the computer in the den and opened up the files I'd copied onto the USB flash drive. A series of spreadsheets showed loans, balance forward, profit, loss, interest payments, dividends, expenses, and more of the same. The balance in the account for Hazelton Holdings was $291,000, and Harbourfront stood a close second at $288,000. How come the cheque for two grand from the chick running those galleries, worth over half a million on paper, had bounced?

It was almost three in the morning by the time I finished reading and trying to make sense of all the financial shenanigans. I was so wired. The only thing that convinced me to finally call it a night was that I wasn't under contract to the Canada Revenue Agency. I could clearly see that something between Darren and his investment business and Christine and her galleries was less than kosher, but it wasn't up to me to go running to the tax man. I told myself that all the intricacies of the transactions really made no difference to me. My only concern was who had killed Gordon, and I truly had no idea if the pages on the computer monitor in front of me had anything to do with his death or not, though it would be hard to think otherwise. The only thing that was certain was that I wasn't going to piece it together tonight.

Best to get out of the skin-tight skirt and the push-up bra that was pretty much bisecting my ribcage and go to bed. I hoped the answers would come to me in my dreams.

# *Friday, April 17, 10:05 a.m.*

"Thank you for seeing me on such short notice, Mrs. Hanes," I said, putting down my china cup of lukewarm dishwater.

My first choice for this morning would have been Mr. Belham, but I hadn't been able to reach him. So, instead, I was sitting in Mrs. Hanes's living room, drinking a cup of tea I didn't really want.

"I'm happy to help you any way I can. It would never have occurred to me to hire an investigator, but now that you're here, I'm so full of hope."

"Remember, I can't make any promises, but I'll give it my very best."

"Thank you, dear. So what is it you'd like from me?"

"I'd like to know more about Christine and Gordon, the engagement, the wedding plans, and the breakup. How long had they dated before they announced plans to marry?"

"I guess a little over two years. Do you really believe the wedding or their relationship has something to do with his death?"

"I'm not sure. It's just suspicious that he died the very same day they planned to marry. Okay, what about their breakup? What was the real reason for it?"

"All he told me was that he wanted to have more time to develop himself. He didn't want to rush into things. He had big plans professionally, and I think his career maybe took on a bit more importance than it should have for someone his age."

"How so?"

"Well, for one thing, in his last few months he took a lot more business trips." Mrs. Hanes took a sip of her tea and then removed an imaginary speck of dust from the coffee table. "Maybe it seemed like he was travelling more than he should have, but keep in mind that until those last few months, all his work was done locally. He never used to go on business trips."

"Where was he travelling to?"

"The Bahamas."

I choked on my tepid tea.

"Are you okay dear? Can I get you a glass of water?"

"No, no, I'm fine." I dabbed the embroidered napkin at my mouth and got lipstick on it. Shit, this looked like antique linen. Would the red slash stain it? "Please continue."

"Gordon said he was thinking of opening a branch office there. I know very little about investing, so I didn't ask much about it. I'm sure if he thought it was smart to expand there, then he'd have made a success of it."

"From what I've learned about Gordon, I think you're right." Proud Mama notwithstanding, the money laundering angle was even more alive and well. I had no idea if it had anything to do with his murder or not, but … I did, however, have several ideas on hold that I'd revisit after I got a little more background from Mr. Belham.

Time to switch gears and see what else I might learn from the matriarch. "I don't mean to pry, but I need to ask you about some other topics. Some of my questions may seem insensitive."

"Don't apologize. The police asked every question that came into their heads and were rather gruff about the whole process. I don't expect much would unsettle me now after all that's been said and done thus far."

I suspected that very few things would elicit anything more than a benign reaction from Mrs. Hanes. As depressing as the topic of our conversation was, she seemed no more emotional than if she were renewing her passport. Bland, blah, bored, boring, blasé, bleary, blurred, bleak. It wasn't as if she didn't care; it just seemed as if all her emotional reserves had been spent.

"Did Gordon have an insurance policy?"

"Of course."

"And who was the beneficiary?"

"I was. The policy was for over one million dollars. I gave it all to charity."

"What about his will?"

"Again he left almost everything to me, but he set aside some funds for Rebecca, and he made some generous bequests to a number of causes he'd always supported. I gave all the money I inherited to a charity to fund cancer research."

"How much did he leave to Rebecca?"

"Half a million dollars, I think."

Who got fuzzy on that much money? *Oh, half mil here, half mil there. I think my niece inherited a five followed by five zeroes, but who knows? It's such a pittance. Chump change really.* And if you could afford to give away a million bucks, then you must have had a very healthy reserve fund to tap into.

"I think I'll need to chat with Rebecca," I said.

"I'm certain she'd be happy to help you."

"Well, that's the thing, Mrs. Hanes. I've spoken to her before, though not about wills and insurance, and she wasn't very receptive."

"I can talk to her and ask her to co-operate." She was now picking imaginary lint off her ivory blouse.

"I'd appreciate that, but I should warn you that it was kind of volatile the last time we met."

"Well, I don't think Rebecca would let me down."

"Okay, I appreciate that, but let's put her aside for now. What about Christine? Did she inherit anything when Gordon died?"

"Not a cent. After they ended their engagement, Gordon changed his insurance policy and his will. Mind you, that doesn't mean he didn't care about her financial well-being."

"What do you mean?"

There was a very long pause before Mrs. Hanes spoke. "I'm not sure I should mention it."

"I respect your privacy, but keep in mind that I can't do my job without having all the information. And in case you aren't sure what's important and what's irrelevant, leave it for me to decide. I protect and respect the confidentiality of the people I meet through my cases. However, you have to be upfront with me."

"Well, I'm sure this is insignificant, but —"

"Like I said, you have to let me decide what's significant and what's not."

"Gordon was still helping Christine financially. He gave her an allowance or a stipend every month. She and her mother have had a tough time financially over the last few years."

"I thought they'd had no contact since they broke up? That's what Christine told me."

"They didn't. He mailed her a series of postdated cheques, and the matter was closed as far as he was concerned."

"How much did he give her?"

"I believe it was four thousand dollars a month. Yes, one thousand a week."

"That's awfully generous of him."

"He was very generous."

"What was his motivation for giving her money? Generous or not, that's a lot of cash to give to someone you've decided not to grow old with."

"I think it was guilt money. He knew she'd have a hard time making ends meet, and he knew she'd have been set with him financially. Don't confuse that as meaning she loved him for his money or wanted to marry him for financial reasons."

"It's really hard not to," I said. Try impossible.

"It wasn't intended as a long-term thing. Gordon just wanted to help her get back on her feet and start a new life without him. He began giving her money when they split up. I think he only intended to help her for a year or so."

"Did she know she was out of his will? Off his insurance policy?"

"Yes. I think part of the impetus for the financial arrangement was that she had indeed spent a fair bit on the wedding that never happened. A lot of things were non-refundable, like the deposit on the banquet hall, the dress, the invitations. He didn't want her to … well, it was bad enough to have a broken heart, but then the money …"

"I see. Speaking of the wedding, tell me whatever you can remember about the plans they had."

"Like what?"

"Where was the ceremony supposed to be? The reception? Had they planned their honeymoon? Anything?" I'd been taking notes all along, but for whatever reason I paid particular attention to her replies about the nullified nuptials.

About an hour later, after going through the wedding scrapbook she'd started when they announced the engagement, I had as much info as I thought I could use. I had no idea what I would use it for, except I now knew just how much planning went into the Big Day. I imagined what it would have been like if Mick and I had stayed together and planned a wedding. I bet Shane and Lindsey would have taken over and turned the whole thing into the party of the century. Good thing I was single.

When I left Mrs. Hanes's house, I walked down to Yonge and Bloor, glad that it was finally sunny again, even though the breeze made it rather nippy. I tried Belham from my cell, and his secretary informed me he was away all day in meetings. Shit. I needed his money sense to walk me through the Darren files.

I stopped for lunch at an Indian buffet restaurant and ate way more than I should have. Who could resist butter chicken and saag paneer? Apparently, I couldn't resist it twice. Nor could I resist pakoras, raita, naan, and mango pudding.

Fortified after a yummy lunch, I was ready to try my luck with Rebecca once again. Mrs. Hanes had said when I was leaving that she was about to phone her niece. I hoped the niece would play nice.

# Friday, 1:40 p.m.

"If it weren't for my aunt, there's no way I'd be speaking to you right now. I think it's horrible to pry into people's lives and I think it's even more horrible to pretend to be something you're not."

I had suggested to Rebecca that we go for a stroll. I didn't want to grab a beverage together and perhaps once again end up with liquid in my face. We were walking through Yorkville, past the big-assed rock that some foolish bureaucrat had paid a lot of money for. The streets were busy with folks taking advantage of the sunny day. A few people were earnestly trying to convince themselves that spring had sprung; some even sat at the tables outside the neighbourhood coffee shops. After a second look, I realized that all the diehards were smokers, puffing away outdoors where the Smoking Police had banished them.

"I think being murdered is pretty horrible," I said.

"It is. Was. But don't you see? Nothing will bring him back. Why don't you just leave us alone so we can move on?"

"Doesn't it bother you that someone got away with murder?"

"Christine got away with murder. It wasn't just 'someone.' It was Christine." Rebecca's voice had taken on a hard edge, her jaw tightening a little.

"I don't know if she killed him or not, but say she did, then she's been getting away with it. If she killed him, shouldn't she be in jail?" I had a momentary visual of Christine in a concrete cellblock, no manicures, no mud wraps, no designer suits even if they were last season's. I recalled her attitude and her mouth, and the trouble both would get her into with the informal prison hierarchy. Hee-hee. Wouldn't be long before she was somebody's bitch.

"I suppose," Rebecca said. "But if the police haven't charged her yet, it's not likely they ever will."

"Speaking of 'will,' I understand Gordon's will left you with five hundred thousand dollars. He left everything else to his mother or to charity. How come you inherited? It's not like you need the money."

"We were close, okay?"

Rebecca and I had walked along Avenue Road, then ended up on Prince Arthur Avenue and passed a lot of beautiful historic buildings that were now home to some of the University of Toronto's fraternities. It looked as if the Delta Kappa Epsilon Omega Whatever groups of rowdy post-secondary boys placed little premium on maintenance and groundskeeping. A shame. Some of the buildings were gorgeous or had been at one time.

Eventually, we found ourselves in a little parkette that might be beautiful in summer when the flowers bloomed and the trees were leafy and children were playing, but on this early spring day it seemed sort of decrepit and lonely. We were the only ones there, aside from a street person sleeping under a ratty quilt on a bench at the opposite side of the erstwhile green space. Rebecca and I sat on a bench whose brown paint was peeling after a winter of snow being dumped on it. I broke the ice after a few minutes of silence.

"I doubt you were that close. It just doesn't fit with everything else. Did the money fund your trips to Freeport? Did you use it to buy a condo or a house there? I find it odd that you never spend money on hotels or restaurants when you go to the Bahamas. Care to enlighten me?"

"How in the name of God do you know all this?"

"Let's talk about you, not me."

"It feels like you've invaded my life. How dare you!"

"Yeah, well, investigating is what I do. Now pop a Paxil or a Percocet and let's get talking. I'm going to be on your ass till I find out what I need to know. I'll hound you at work, I'll follow you to Freeport, I'll speak to your friends and associates and even your doctors, and I'll make myself one helluva giant pain in the ass and you'll eventually tell me what I want to know to finally get rid of me."

Neither of us spoke for what seemed like several minutes. The only sound punctuating the stony silence was an abrupt symphony of flatulence from the wino on the park bench. He sat up and took a swig out of his bottle, then belched and flopped back down on the bench.

"His son, Ephraim." Her voice was very soft and her eyes were focused on her hands, which were fidgeting on her lap.

"Pardon?" I said, my eyes widening.

"Ephraim. Gordon has a son. Ephraim lives with his mother in Freeport. The money I inherited was to help him."

"Tell me more. Who's Ephraim's mother? How old is the boy? Where did this kid come from?" Obviously, I didn't mean the last question in a physiological sense.

"It was one of those things that happen. Spring break during Gordon's last year of university. A fling with a local girl. Unexpected pregnancy. Gordon was just about to graduate and begin his career. A baby out of wedlock would have destroyed his life."

"In this day and age it's not such a big deal. And it's not like Gordon was a teenager. What would he have been at the end of university? Twenty-one? Twenty-two? Good God, lots of people become parents under much more difficult circumstances."

"Well, he didn't love the woman. There was no way he was going to marry her. He wasn't even sure at first that the baby was his."

"Obviously, he did an about-face on that. Tell me the whole story." I was shocked. I figured Rebecca had some secrets, I figured funny money was a key plot in the Bahamas story, I had even fleetingly thought there was a drug angle tied into the trips to Freeport, but a baby? A son? Never even crossed my mind.

"Gordon swore me to secrecy. I've never told anyone what I'm about to tell you."

"Yeah, well, murder changes the game. The dead don't have secrets." Pretty spiffy line, eh?

"It began like a bad movie. Gordon had a fling with a girl who worked at the resort. He got a panicky phone call about a month after his trip. He didn't believe her. He flew back to the Bahamas when the baby was born, they had some tests done, and sure enough, just after he turned twenty-three, Gordon found out he was a daddy. By this time, after a series of phone calls and emails, whatever, Gordon had come to the conclusion that not only would he not marry this woman but he didn't even like her. A drunk night after a day of playing nine holes, then nine months later a human being he never planned to create now existed."

"Wow!"

"Yes, wow."

"So what next?" I asked. "Why are you involved?"

"I suppose I need to back up a bit and tell you the whole story."

"That would be refreshing." *Oops!* I hadn't meant that to sound as sarcastic as it had.

Rebecca gave me a stern look and continued. "It took a while to establish paternity in those days. 'In those days' makes it sound historic, but really, eleven years ago, technology was nothing like it is today, and things move even more slowly in the Caribbean."

"I see."

"By the time they established that the baby was his, the animosity was untenable. I think Gordon disliked the mother so much that it overshadowed whatever feelings he might have had for his son. They both got lawyers and they fought it out in the Bahamian courts. That took a while. By then, to Gordon, Ephraim didn't seem so much like his own flesh and blood, but rather a footnote in a testy legal proceeding."

"Poor kid."

Neither of us spoke for a moment or two.

Rebecca stared at the ground, then finally spoke. "Gordon saw Ephraim as a source of stress. He faked a lot of golf trips to get down to Freeport for the court dates and lawyer meetings. Gordon really had to juggle things to sort out the mess. He kept the whole story secret from everyone, even me at first."

"So what changed? He left money to you for the boy's care and you go down to visit?" I was really winging it now. Nothing in my dreams or musings had suggested the story would spin off in this unexpected direction.

Rebecca shoved her hands into her pockets. "I used to smoke, and right now I wish I still did."

"Do you want to go somewhere for a coffee or a drink? Is it getting too cold?" When we were walking, the cool, sunny day had seemed refreshing, but being sedentary, sitting on the park bench with no trees to filter the breeze made it seem a lot colder.

"Let's just walk again. I don't think I want to be inside yet."

"Do you have to get back to work soon?"

"No. I told them I had to leave for a family emergency. I guess, in a way, that's kind of true."

"Sorry. I know this is upsetting. Believe me, I wouldn't be asking questions if I didn't somehow think they'd help me find answers."

"I guess so. Eventually, Gordon and Ephraim's mother came to an agreement about child support. He sent money every month. She'd occasionally send photographs that Gordon never wanted to see. It went on that way for years."

So Gordon was forking over a hefty sum every month to a kid he'd never wanted and to a woman he'd refused to marry. That either made him a very generous and decent human being or a great big hapless sap, or the mother had had a very good lawyer. If I hadn't known better, I'd have thought he'd faked his own death just to get out of the monthly financial commitments. Between this and Darren, it sure seemed as if Gordon was a lot more valuable alive than dead.

"So what changed?" I asked.

"Ephraim. He was getting older and started asking about his daddy. He also began asking about his heritage. He was so much lighter than the other boys at school."

Of course. I didn't know why it hadn't occurred to me, but, yes, the mother would have been black. A light bulb went on above my head. "Back up. Are you saying that race had something to do with the rejection of his son? In this day and age? You can't be serious."

"Race was never an issue for Gordon. He obviously slept with a black woman, didn't he?"

"Yeah, and so did Thomas Jefferson and so did Senator Strom Thurmond." It was difficult to keep myself from sounding judgmental. Horniness had little to do with being culturally inclusive, unless you thought of it in terms of an equal-opportunity penis.

"Don't look at it that way. There's more to it than that. The woman is trash. Blue-collar, lowbrow trash. She clearly hoped to find a meal ticket in some tourist and get sponsored to Canada or the States. She was a high-school drop-out, a barmaid. They had nothing in common except a one-night stand."

"So what else? Keep talking."

"This will be hard for you to understand, but Gordon could have accepted a mixed-race baby. He would even have been happy in a biracial relationship if he'd ever fallen in love with a black woman or an Asian woman or whatever. It's the generation above us that has a problem with it, and admittedly, so do some of the younger folks. Look at Rosedale. It's lily-white. Look at the members of the Granite Club. Look at the backgrounds we all have — British roots. Look at the private schools we all attended. Gloucester Prep has two black kids in it now, but there were no minorities attending it when I was a student. None of the kids when I was growing up were different from me. They were all WASPs."

"This is ridiculous. Are we in Alabama in the fifties? I don't care how you label it or justify it. It's still racism."

"I'm just telling you how it was, what Gordon was thinking. He talked to me about it and he really wrestled with things. It would have been a mess if he'd brought it out in the open. It wouldn't have been fair to the boy, either."

"What about Ephraim's mother? She's a person, too."

"I know. Anyway, Gordon kept the whole thing secret from everyone but me. He sent the monthly cheque and that was it. Then, about two years ago, Ephraim started asking about his daddy and life in Canada. He phoned Gordon a few times and said he wanted to visit. Imagine, if all of a sudden an eleven-year-old mulatto boy had arrived on the scene?"

"My goodness, what would people think?" I didn't even try to hide the sarcasm in my voice.

"Please try not to be judgmental. You never met Gordon, and you'd know if you had that he was a good person. Race had less to do with it than he just simply didn't like the boy's mother. And Gordie came through financially and eventually he came through emotionally. In the last year of his life he saw Ephraim several times. I went with him on a couple of trips. Ephraim was so excited about the visits from his Canadian daddy and his aunt. Then there was the trip when I had to tell him his daddy was dead."

"That must have been hard."

"You have no idea."

We talked a while longer about the kid who liked collecting seashells and kept scraping his knees after skateboarding accidents. He loved the water and loved to swim and dreamed of becoming a marine biologist.

"I'm his only connection to his father," Rebecca said. "I can't replace him nor can I make up for those lost years, but I can still do right by him. That's why I visit every month and that's why it's secret."

"So who's the financial adviser Terry Snider and how does he fit into all this?"

"Terry's a she, not a he, and Teresa is the boy's mother. Gordon helped her get started in investments, not as a partner but as an employee. He didn't want his son raised by a woman who worked nights in a bar and wasn't there for her son."

"Oh."

We chatted a while longer, or at least Rebecca did. I just sat and listened. Maybe there was no funny money angle, after all. Or maybe there was. Damn it! I needed to talk with Belham. The money thing was as clear as mud, and he was the only person who could explain it to me.

I walked with Rebecca back to the garage where she'd parked, and we said goodbye on much more civil terms than after out last meeting, though I didn't think she'd be adding my name to her Christmas card list.

Now my head was as full as my still-bursting belly, and I didn't know if I had more questions after that exchange or more answers.

What next? Darren? Ted? Christine? Too bad I didn't have a crystal ball. I walked south along Yonge Street, past my office, past a bunch of dollar stores and discount clothing shops. The bargains in the store windows didn't register. I passed some shoe stores and record shops and didn't feel inspired to go inside and browse. I ignored the magazine stores and coffee shops and didn't pay attention to the punks trying to score E in front of the 7-Eleven. Nor did I really notice the panhandlers who, more and more aggressively, asked me for spare change. I cranked up the tunes on my MP3 player and let Green Day, Franz Ferdinand, and The White Stripes do their best to distract me from the whirlpool of thoughts eddying in my cerebellum.

I noticed that in this block and the next there were a number of psychics offering everything from reading tea leaves to numerology to palm reading. Most of the charlatans had signs on the sidewalk offering their services, some for as little as five dollars. It occurred to me that half a sawbuck was too low a price to reveal the secrets of the past and the future. It also seemed that for five bucks I had nothing much to lose.

## *Friday, 2:41 p.m.*

I called Lindsey on her cell. She was showing potential clients some fully detached homes on the Kingsway, but could meet me later for a drink. I tried Belham's secretary again, and no, he hadn't had a change in plans and returned unexpectedly to the office, and yes, she had given him my messages. It wasn't a good time to drop by to see Shane; at this time of day he was knee-deep preparing the nightly featured dishes. That left Ted Chapman, Darren, or Christine. Of course, I could always forget about all that and show up for my shift tonight at the orgasms on call centre. I faked a cold and called in sick; I was way too wrapped up in this case to talk dirty to people who couldn't get dates.

Back to deciding whose ear to bend next or whom to submit to my oh-so-gentle inquisition. Given the choice between a man from whose body I'd love to lick melted chocolate, a surly prick with an attitude who might or might not hit me or hit on me, or an ice queen bitch from hell, was there really any doubt what option I'd pick?

Darren must have had a sixth sense about me because he looked toward the door as soon as I entered. I flashed a brief and flagrantly insincere smile his way and took my usual perch at the counter.

I had tried phoning Ted first and had gotten his voice mail. I had left a message and asked him to call me on my cell number. Not wanting to piss away an afternoon and indecisive about whether to try Darren or Christine next, I'd kept walking until I'd found myself within a few blocks of Pockets, the billiard place. I guess, subconsciously, I had headed in the opposite direction of Christine's Hazelton gallery, though to tell the truth,

I wasn't very far from her Harbourfront gallery. Given a choice between them, Darren gave me a rash but Christine equalled blistering hives.

I was about two blocks from the pool hall when I finally admitted to myself I was going there. In the short walk between the decision and crossing the threshold of Darren's billiard sanctuary, I'd come up with a plan. With or without Belham's financial explanations and advice, it was time to tackle Darren. And since I had nothing but gut instinct to go on and not a clue what I was talking about, I decided to bluff my way through our rendezvous. Chutzpah, work your magic.

As Belham had said, the best defence was a good offence.

Darren was talking to a man with salt-and-pepper hair and a nice suit. The companion had his back to me, and Darren saw me over the other guy's shoulder. "What the hell do you want?"

My presence clearly irritated Darren; he hadn't even waited till the end of his conversation to come over and bark at me.

"What the fuck?" Darren croaked. "You think I offed my cousin so I could make a few thousand bucks? Are you insane?"

Darren had immediately aborted his tête-à-tête with the gentleman he'd been talking to. We left the pool hall and went to a divey Jamaican tavern across the street. There was absolutely no chance that either of us would be seen here by anyone we knew. A chalkboard menu announced the daily special: goat curry with steamed callaloo and rice for $4.99. We sat across from each other at a scarred turquoise Formica table, drinking Red Stripe beer out of the bottle. In a different milieu the decor might have been considered kitschy shabby chic, but here it just looked tacky.

"Darren, I know all about your partnership with Christine. I know she's helping you hide the cash from selling drugs."

"Selling drugs? What the fuck are you talking about?"

I had no idea what I was talking about but rattling his cage was kind of fun. "Oh, come on it's obvious. You spend all afternoon at Pockets and drive a fully loaded Jaguar. You haven't got even half the brains Gordon did and you sure as hell aren't the investor he was. Admit it, Pockets is where you retail your products." His face was getting red, and I thought for sure he'd hit me. I backed my chair up a few inches. Hmm ... maybe this wasn't so much fun.

"You're crazy. Fucking crazy. Is it that time of the month or something? You got PMS and want to make me miserable? I don't fucking believe this."

"Gordon was ready to blow the whistle on you, so you killed him to shut him up."

"You know what, you little bitch? This is harassment and slander and you'll be hearing from my lawyer real fucking soon."

"Then where did the $291K in Hazelton Holdings come from? And what about the $288K in the Harbourfront account?"

"What do you mean?" His face dropped, and I knew I'd more than hit a nerve. It was the first time he'd uttered a sentence without using *fucking* as a participial adjective. My goodness, he was too stunned to swear.

I continued. "Christine's fudging the books for the sales at her galleries. She's dummying the numbers to show a loss. You're buying art for way more than it's worth. The money is split between you, and you're watching it grow as a result of a lot of shady stock trades. You could both go to jail. Fraud. Tax evasion. The list goes on. The game's over, Darren."

"You have no idea what you're talking about."

That was certainly true, but it didn't stop me. "Gordon knew what was going on, and he died because of it. But I've already told everything I know to my lawyer and to another friend. If anything happens to me, the cops will be all over you like flies on shit."

I had mustered every ounce of bravado for that speech and had given a performance worthy of an Oscar. Half of all I'd said was bullshit, half was supposition, half was a hunch, and the other half was improvisation. And yes, I knew I should have said quarters. And maybe one more half was horseshoe-up-the-ass-lucky guessing.

"I didn't kill him," Darren said.

"What in the hell makes you think I'd believe you?"

"The night, well, morning he was killed, I have an alibi."

"And that was —"

"It's really none of your fucking business, but I was in jail. Just for the night. I'd been in a fight in a bar on College Street. It was after last call and some wanker was asking for it. Cops picked me up for drunk and disorderly. I spent the night in the drunk tank at Broadview and Gerrard. They released me at nine the next morning."

"Doesn't mean you couldn't have paid someone to do it."

"But it doesn't mean I did, either."

Gee, it was hard to find holes in that logic. There was a pause while he took a swig of his beer, and I followed suit.

"You aren't working with the police on this, are you?" Darren asked.

"That depends on what you tell me. Drug dealing pisses me off. The scum who do that belong in jail."

"It's not drugs. I'm just trying to help Christine, and I'm being paid quite well for my assistance. She's going to file for fucking bankruptcy very soon."

"And?"

"Bankruptcy will leave her with nothing. I'm helping her hide a little nest egg. The fucking debts are mostly her mothers, mostly from gambling, but that doesn't matter to her creditors. The galleries are in both their names — mother and daughter are listed as partners. Creditors don't fucking care which partner pays the invoices as long as they get their money. She's trying to move whatever she can away from the company before she files for bankruptcy."

"What's in it for you?"

"I get twenty-five percent of it all. And it's a way for me to wash the money I shouldn't have made off some other trades."

"Graduated from the Martha Stewart School of Stock Trading, did we?"

"It's only illegal if you get caught. We didn't start any of this till after Gordon died. As long as he was alive, he could help Christine out. And as long as he was alive, our firm was making decent money. It's been a little tough without him. I've had to call in a few informational favours."

And that was the end of that. I believed he hadn't killed Gordon. I believed his motive for partnering with Christine was money. I believed he'd been in jail the night of the murder, and that was easy enough to check, anyway. And I didn't believe he was selling drugs. That line had just been a good cattle prod to get him to talk.

So then who had killed Gordon and why?

# Friday, 6:10 p.m.

Masoud was bartending tonight at the Pilot, and when he was at the helm, martinis were the order of the day. I was sipping a Cosmopolitan and waiting very impatiently for Lindsey. She arrived just as I was contemplating ordering another cocktail.

"Make it two, Masoud. Those are so yummy." She turned to me and said, "After the afternoon I've had, I deserve a drink, but just one. I have to drive."

"What was so bad about your afternoon?"

"The usual real-estate agent woes. Losers who want the perfect house but can't even get approved for a mortgage on a mobile home. Dreamers who think a starter home means five bedrooms and an in-ground pool. Time bandits who get me to run them all over the city looking at houses they can't afford."

"Sucks."

"What about you? How's the Mystery of the Fatal Fiancée going?"

"I'd rather be showing bungalows to young families on a fixed income."

"That bad, huh?"

"Yup."

I filled Lindsey in on all the events since we'd gone to the funeral. She listened attentively and didn't even interrupt to ask questions until after I'd finished my malice-and-mayhem monologue.

"So let me get this straight. Darren's an asshole, but not a killer. Christine's a sneaky lying bitch, but not a killer. Rebecca's a stoned auntie, but not a killer. There are no drugs, but prescribed ones. There's lots of art fraud and tax evasion, but no offshore banking. And there's a son of mixed race in the Bahamas. Does that just about cover it?"

"Yup," I answered. "More or less."

"And Ted? What's the update on him?"

"I left a voice mail on his —" My cell twittered to life. I pulled it out of my bag and looked at the call display. "Oh, my God, it's him!"

"Who?"

"It's Ted. One sec." I flipped open the phone while walking to the front entrance. It was way too noisy in the bar to talk on the phone without yelling and looking like one of those self-important jackasses who mistakenly thinks the whole establishment enjoys listening to his end of a cell phone conversation.

"Hi, Sasha, it's Ted. Sorry it took me so long to get back to you. I was on the go all day schmoozing clients from out of town. What a drag."

"Not to worry, Ted. It wasn't urgent."

"I'd love to hear what you've learned so far. Can we meet for a drink?"

"Um, well, I'm actually having one now. A friend met me at the Pilot for a quick drink. How about if we meet in an hour?"

"The Pilot? I haven't been there in ages. Why don't I join you and your friend?"

"Sure. We're sitting at the bar."

"Great. See you in about ten minutes."

When I got back to my bar stool, I said to Lindsey, "Do these jeans make my ass look fat?"

"No. You look fine. Why?"

"How about the hair? And lipstick." I dug through my purse trying to find the million-dollar ruby gloss I'd bought at Chadwick's. Wallet, keys, MP3 player. No makeup at all. "Do you have any on you? Anything bright red?"

"Who are you ... oh, wait, Ted? He's on his way here?"

"Yup."

"Tuck in your shirt and undo the top button."

Ten minutes later Ted walked in, and Lindsey and I casually waved him over to the table we'd moved to in our friend Jessica's section. Lindsey practically drooled on Ted's shoes when I introduced them, and Jessica's eyes almost popped out of her head.

"I'll have a Heineken. Girls? Ready for another?"

"Sure," we said in unison.

Jessica smiled and went off to the bar to fill our order.

"So tell me what you've been up to," Ted said as he draped his sports coat over the back of his chair and loosened his tie.

"It's hard to even know where to begin." I finished the last sip of my drink just as Jessica arrived with the next round. I left the drink untouched while I gave Ted a quick-and-dirty lowdown of the past couple of days.

"A son?" Ted said when I finished my update. "Eleven years old? I had no idea. Wow! We have to tell Mrs. Hanes."

"Just a reminder, Ted. I told you because you're my client, but it's not up to me to tell Mrs. Hanes."

"I think you should tell her about him," Lindsey piped in. "She'll probably be thrilled to find out she has a grandson."

"If you decide to do that, Ted, you'd best talk it over with Rebecca first," I said.

"God, this is a lot to chew on," Ted said. "Is there anything else I should know?"

I told him a carefully edited version of the Darren and Christine partnership. As much as I disliked both of them, I had next to no proof for much of it and had gleaned a lot of the story by guesswork that Darren had mostly filled in. The statements I'd pilfered from his office showed only how much money was in the account, but didn't quite yet exactly one hundred percent definitely prove where the money had come from, and I needed to fill in that piece of the puzzle. It wouldn't be smart to shoot my mouth off just yet, especially since I didn't understand it well enough to explain it.

"It's always a question of motive and who benefits." I paused for a moment and took a sip of my drink. "The bottom line is that I really don't think any of them killed him. It doesn't fit. I wish it did, because to tell you the truth, I'm running out of theories."

"Theories? What kind of theories. Conspiracy theories? Scientific ones? Legal —"

Oh-oh. I knew that Adenoids in Overdrive voice anywhere. "Victor, what brings you here?"

Without being asked, Victor grabbed the empty seat at our table, which of course happened to be right next to me. Being so close to him, I noticed his scent, a mixture of Old Spice and sulphur. About the only thing sexier than the smell was his plaid flannel shirt and bottle-green gabardine pleated chinos, again with white sports socks and black Gucci loafers.

"Hey, waitress, can you bring me a ginger ale and another round for the table?"

Lindsey looked mortified at the way Victor called out the order to Jessica, who was serving a table on the opposite side of the room. Jess, to her credit, took it in stride, but I'd wager she'd be serving Victor's drink in a dirty glass. I downed my Cosmopolitan in one big gulp.

Ted politely exchanged pleasantries with the new arrival. "So, Victor, what brings you here?"

"Well, I remembered that Sasha sometimes hangs out here, being so close to her office and all, and I know that most people like to have a drink at happy hour, especially on Fridays, and I was just a few blocks away and thought I could drop by and see who was here and —"

"And here I am," I cut in. "Sorry, Victor, I don't mean to be rude, but this is kind of a business meeting. One drink with you and then we'll have to get back to work."

Victor meant well, and he really was kind of sweet in a sort of dorky way, but all that aside, I was starting to think about a restraining order. He was popping up a bit too much lately for my liking.

"How did things go with Christine?" Ted asked.

I tried to kick Ted under the table, but got Lindsey instead.

"Ouch, what was that for?"

"Sorry, Linds, muscle spasm."

It was too late to derail Ted's line of conversation.

"Have you taken her out to dinner yet?" he asked Victor.

"No, well, you know, I went to the gallery to see her twice and both times she was abrupt, actually kind of rude. She's beautiful and seems very intelligent, but I can't abide somebody who treats people like she does. You know, I even brought her a little gift both times. The first day I brought flowers and the next day a big box of chocolates —"

"That's so sweet of you," Lindsey said.

She had only briefly met Victor once a few months ago, right around the height of his divorce and the height of his depression. Or should that be the low of his depression? Whatever. She'd never seen him in motor-mouth mode.

"I'd planned a nice dinner date for us at Duke's Buffet —"

"Excuse me," I said abruptly. "I have to go to the ladies' room." I planned to lock myself in a stall and bang my head against the walls till I was numb. Perhaps I stayed in the washroom too long. By the time I returned to our table, Ted was gone.

"He got a call," Lindsey told me. "Said it was an 'urgent personal matter' and split."

"Here you go," Jessica said as she placed yet another round of drinks on our table. "That Incredible Hunk bought another round for you on his way out."

"Guess I'm leaving my car in the lot and staying at your place tonight," Lindsey said.

"Shane will be glad."

Victor jumped in. "Hey, so now that your client's gone, I guess you don't have business to discuss. Great, we can have a grand old time talking about this, that, and the other thing. I haven't had much of a chance to get to know you, Lindsey. Tell me all about yourself, where are you from, are you single, who's Shane? Oh, wait, he's your brother, right, Sasha?" Victor hoisted his glass. "Here's to a good night out with good friends. Cheers, everyone."

Kill me now.

## Saturday, April 18, 10:15 a.m.

Lindsey and I had sat up talking quite late until Shane had come home just after two in the morning. We had been stuck with Victor for another hour before I'd said something about menstrual cramps and that time of the month, then Lindsey and I had bolted. Back at my place, sitting around the kitchen table, we'd talked some more about the case while filling our faces with grilled cheese sandwiches.

I'd slept until almost ten o'clock and gotten up to an empty house. Shane must have gone to the St. Lawrence Market on his usual Saturday morning quest for fresh produce. And Lindsey must have gone off for a day of showing "fixer uppers" and "handyman's dreams" to potential buyers.

With a busy day in store for myself, I decided to get the most unpleasant task out of the way first. I picked up the phone, secretly hoping there would be no dial tone.

"Hi, Christine. It's me, Sasha."

"Yes?"

Well, she hadn't immediately hung up on me, so that was a good sign. "I think we should talk. About Gordon."

"Can it wait? I have a lot on my agenda for today." Her voice had all the warmth of the metal stirrups at an OB-GYN's office. I had expected as much and wasn't surprised that she tried to blow me off.

"It's important. At least I think it is. Can I meet you at the gallery? It won't take long."

"Fine. I'll be at the Harbourfront gallery by eleven. I'll see you then. For no more than ten minutes."

"Great. Thank you." I kept my voice as cheery as I could, though from the comfort and privacy of my living room I was giving her the finger.

---

"Here, Christine, see? I've made it as easy as possible for you." I handed her the page I'd printed off my computer at home.

"Why do you want to know all this?" she asked as she glanced at the list of fill-in-the-blank questions on the paper.

"I keep coming back to the wedding. He was killed on the day you were supposed to marry. And I keep ruling everything else out."

The thread Lindsey and I had kept coming back to during our late-night powwow was the wedding.

Christine scanned the page. "Caterer, DJ, limo service, florist, photographer. "I can give you most of the names, but don't ask me for contact info."

"Not to worry. I can look that up myself. I just need the names."

"Shouldn't matter, anyway, because the wedding planner should have all that info on file unless she tossed it all when the wedding was called off." She prattled on as she filled in whatever info she could recall. I tried to seem as if I was mesmerized by the artwork on display, but soapstone carving really wasn't my thing. I studied some of the price tags and decided even more that Inuit sculpture really wasn't my thing.

Then I feigned interest in the vividly coloured landscape paintings that adorned the walls. Some of them were really quite breathtaking: shades of oranges and blues brought to life the crisp sunrises and sunsets of our northern skies. I didn't even bother to look at their price tags.

Another wall showcased a series of First Nations paintings and drawings, but they really weren't my cup of tea, either. The pictures were all about negative space and broad white backgrounds with simple curved lines depicting wildlife and aboriginal folklore. The lines were all sparse and sleek and the colours were restricted to two or three hues. I recognized a few of the paintings and names from the Woodland Indian art movement that I had learned about way back when I'd taken Canadian social studies in Ms. Hanlon's grade eight class. I figured the pictures were nice, sort of mystic and primitive, but I just didn't get them.

"Is that it?" Christine asked a few minutes later.

"Yup."

"Here you go then." She folded the paper and handed it back to me.

"Thank you. See? I told you it would be quick."

---

Task number two was a visit to the Metro Reference Library, which was back uptown. I had to hurry, since I had another trek to make later today. But first, I had a hunch and had to do a bit of research.

How come in movies the library archives were always in some dark and gloomy basement? The lower level of the Toronto Reference Library had microfilm copies of all the local newspapers, in some cases dating back more than a hundred years. And, like in movies, the only people in the newspaper archives were a bunch of pasty-faced, bespectacled research rats earnestly poring over the words in front of them.

I got the microfilm for the past two years of the *Toronto Star* and the *Toronto Sun*. Without knowing the exact details I knew exactly what I was looking for. Within an hour I had found it, not once, but twice. I printed copies of all the relevant news stories and left.

Next up was a visit to Angela Livingstone, whom I had called last night. A call to directory assistance had gotten me her number. She had certainly seemed intrigued by my call and was willing to meet with me today, but I had to travel out to her bailiwick.

So now I had to get my ass back downtown to the train station, a short hop from where I'd met with Christine an hour and a half ago. I grabbed a hot dog from a street vendor and wolfed it down as I made my way to Union Station.

I bought a round-trip ticket to Burlington, took a window seat, and opened the newspaper to the comics page. Marmaduke was still an untrained, annoying big dog, and I didn't understand why the strip was still syndicated. Cathy was still plump and dowdy and insecure and dateless, and I wondered why that comic strip hadn't been axed, too. An hour later Angela met me at the railway station and we walked a few blocks till we found a Starbucks where we could sit and talk undisturbed.

She ordered a lemon tea, and I followed suit. I figured I could skip the sugar and caffeine for once.

"Are any of the names on this list familiar?" I asked, handing Angela the page of questions Christine had filled in. She took a pair of reading glasses out of her macramé purse. The tortoiseshell-framed glasses made her look very girl-next-door-ish.

"Just this one. Valerie O'Connor was the wedding planner Jeffrey and I had planned to use. Why?"

"What was the date you and Jeff had originally planned for your wedding?"

"April 11. Why?"

"That's the same day he was killed."

"I know. Our rescheduled wedding date was going to be May 23, the Saturday of the Victoria Day weekend. We were keeping things hush-hush. Just me, Jeff and two witnesses, a no-frills chapel in Niagara Falls, and done, I now pronounce you man and wife. No fuss, no muss."

"Is that what made you call it off the first time?"

"Yes, we broke up at the end of January. Christmas had been stressful." I noticed a slight lisp as she said this. "His parents, my parents, trying to get around and see everyone, having turkey dinner with both families, pleasing everyone. We spent a fortune on gifts we couldn't really afford. And through it all, at every family gathering, we got advice and suggestions and conditions about the wedding plans." She blew on her tea before taking a sip.

"I'm sure it was all well intended," I said.

"Of course, it was, but it was so stressful. His mother didn't like the colour scheme I'd picked out. My mother disapproved of the place we chose for the bridal registry. And the bossiness of the whole lot of them." She spoke in a whiny, nasal twang. "'You can't use the same banquet hall cousin Patty used.' 'Nicola McCall had five bridesmaids, you have to have at least six.' 'If you invite Uncle Neil, I'm not coming.' 'Make sure the seating plan for dinner has Matthew as far away from Graham as possible.' And on and on and on. It was horrible, and Jeff and I started bickering constantly about it all. He broke up with me."

"Yikes! I guess I should keep all this in mind if I ever decide to marry."

"Trust me. You're better off eloping."

"So how did the two of you get back on track?"

"After being apart for three or four weeks, we got together for a coffee. He'd been missing me and I was going crazy without him. I was so bitchy during those few weeks. We had a really good heart-to-heart talk and realized we still loved each other." She was blinking back tears while she spoke. "It was the wedding plans and our families that caused the problems. We got back together but kept it all hush-hush. And we decided that we were going to get married our way quietly. And then he was killed, goddamn it!"

At that point the floodgates opened. I ran up to the counter and grabbed a stack of paper napkins because, of course, I didn't have any Kleenex in my purse. She started sobbing loudly, and a few patrons looked over and then studiously turned away.

Poor girl. I couldn't imagine how she felt. I held her hand for a moment, and she let the tears run their course. I was a stranger to her and had no idea how to handle such public private grief. After a while, she excused herself and went to the ladies' room.

"I'm sorry," Angela said when she returned. "I didn't mean to have a meltdown like that. I just couldn't stop it." Her eyes were still red and puffy.

"Don't apologize. You've been on quite the emotional roller coaster recently. I'm so sorry. I can't imagine how it feels." No matter what I chose to say, it was bound to sound clichéd. "As I told you, I'm a private investigator. I've been working on another case that might have something to do with Jeffrey's death."

"Really?" Her face contorted into a mixture of hope and anguish. "The police think it was just random. I have no idea what to think."

"Well, listen up for a minute. Maybe by the end of this you'll think I'm crazy." I took a sip of my still-too-hot tea before I began. Why did some restaurants think that singeing the roof of your mouth was a criterion for a good cuppa? "In the case I'm working on, the victim, also male, had called off his engagement."

"That can't be that uncommon in a city this size, in this day and age. Most people I know are scared at the idea of tying the knot and just want to live together."

I nodded. "That might be true, but the other victim was killed on the date he and the bride-to-be had planned for their wedding. Just like you and Jeffrey."

"Oh, my God!"

"I'd chalk it all up to coincidence, except there's one more parallel between my case and Jeffrey's death."

"I have a feeling I'm not going to like this."

"They had been using the same wedding planner as you."

"You're kidding. Valerie O'Connor?"

"Yup."

"Well, she's one of the best. Her reputation's outstanding, and she really does think of everything. A lot of brides, well, couples, speak very highly of her."

"Well, coincidences and flukes do sometimes happen. People get struck by lightning, sometimes more than once. And you're right. It could be that you both picked her because she's got such a good name. It just makes me wonder what connection there might be between Jeffrey and my client. I don't want to jump to conclusions, but I'm going to dig into the wedding angle."

"Why don't you go to the police with this?"

"I will eventually, but not just yet. I need something a little more concrete."

# Saturday, 7:00 p.m.

After I left Angela, I had to wait for almost an hour for the return train to the city. Once there I had to figure out what to do. I decided to go to the office instead of returning home. Sometimes just being in the office got me into a different, more productive headspace. But when I approached my office, I knew I wouldn't be able to get any work done.

*Son of a bitch!* It was trashed. Top to bottom, inside and out, trashed.

I'd known something was wrong the second I'd approached the office door, since it was open about an inch.

*Shit!*

The jug with the long-since-wilted roses from Victor was smashed, the water making *squooshy* noises under that part of the carpet. My desk chair had been slashed, and the filing cabinets had been tipped over. The garbage bin and recycling box had both been upended. The phone was off the hook, making a beeping noise. My computer, no ... not my computer ... my dearly beloved, late computer, *oh, fuck!*

What was a gal to do? What should I do? I didn't know whether to stay there and clean up or call the cops and report a break-in. I didn't want to be alone and I really wished for once that Victor would put in one of his surprise appearances.

I called Lindsey but got her voice mail. There was no point bothering my brother at work. By this time, I was more than halfway to crying, less from fear than from frustration and anger. Bastards! I could page Dad, but what would be the point? I thought of Victor and knew that if I ever needed him for any favour — large or small — he'd be there in a heartbeat. But I just didn't feel like seeing him today.

I bit the bullet and called the one person I swore I'd never talk to again: Mick Houghton, my ex–lead guitarist and the ex-boyfriend I'd deliberately erased from my memory. Or had tried to.

"Hey, it's me," I said into the phone.

"Whoa! How've you been? What's up?"

Mick, of course, seemed thrilled at the sound of my voice. He had never wanted to break up, and at times I had thought I didn't want to break up, either. He had tried several times in the months that had followed to reconcile, and I'd been tempted.

Eventually, I had just started screening his calls and avoiding him altogether. I skipped parties I knew he'd attend and steered clear of bars or events where he might have a gig. It was too emotionally confusing to see him. Even worse, I wondered if I'd see him with another girl. I had no idea why, but that thought made me jealous.

There was attraction, genuine fondness, and trust, and Mick and I really did care a lot about each other. But we had never gotten along that well, at least not for any length of time. We had dated for about two and a half years and had spent more than half of that time fighting, bickering, making up, and doing it all again the next day. Eventually, my nerves had had enough of the pendulum and I had quit the relationship. And the band.

That was another reason why I had given up on music. Mick and I had played together for years before we started dating. That might have given us a false indication of compatibility. When it came to music, we were completely in tune with each other — pardon the pun — but that synergy had never lasted long once we got offstage. Except, of course, if we were in the bedroom, but that wasn't enough to sustain a relationship, even if we did make beautiful music together, literally and figuratively. God, what a sticky sweet sentiment!

"Mick, I'm sorry to bug you, but I need help," I now said to him.

"Sure, what's up?"

"Can you meet me at my office? I'll wait for you out front."

"Okay. What's wrong? Are you okay?"

"Yeah, yeah, I'm fine. I'm not sick or anything. But something's wrong."

"I'll be there in twenty minutes."

"Thank you."

I fled my office and went to the pizza joint a few doors down where I ate a cardboard slice of stale, all-dressed pizza while I waited for Mick. I hadn't seen him in almost a year and I was nervous. Maybe I shouldn't have called him. Maybe I shouldn't have eaten pizza. I was positive there was something green stuck between my teeth and that my breath now reeked of garlic. A few minutes later the roar of his beat-up, antique Harley announced his arrival, and my heart skipped a beat. That was just fear, though, right?

---

"What the fuck!" Mick said. "This place looks like a Tasmanian devil had an epileptic seizure in it. Thank God you weren't here when it happened. You could've been hurt."

"I don't even want to think about that."

"What's missing? Any idea who did this? What do you think they were looking for?"

"I can offer several guesses, but that's it. I have some valuable files, paper ones and computer files, but they're all at home."

"Have you been home yet?"

"Nope."

"Is your dad in town?"

"Nope."

"And I bet Shane's at work?"

"Yup."

"Let's go. I brought an extra helmet."

I was never the motorcycle aficionado that Mick was, and to me April was still too early to be riding. The wind was biting as it whipped my hair into my face, and my hands, sans gloves, felt like ice. I focused on wiggling my fingers to keep the blood circulating in my extremities, and to prevent me from pondering how nice it was to sit behind Mick, my legs wrapped around him, and … *stop that line of thinking! Don't go there. No way.* I'd been down that road before and it led to a lot of tears. Never again. But still …

When we got to my house and did a walk-through, everything seemed intact.

"So what the hell kind of case are you working on?" Mick asked.

"You don't want to know."

"How do you know they won't try to find whatever they're looking for here? Maybe Shane will stay at Lindsey's tonight. I don't think you should be alone."

"Shit, I hadn't thought of that."

"Well, give me the background. What's it all about?"

I gave Mick a rundown of the Gordon file and bitter brides and the most recent developments after my visits to the library and to Burlington. The whole thing came pouring out in one long, jumbled breath.

"Slow down."

"Don't tell me what to do."

"You know what I meant," he said. "How about a drink?"

I nodded, and Mick went to the liquor cabinet and fixed us a couple of rum and Cokes.

"So the Burlington chick and this Christine broad both used the same wedding planner?" He plopped himself beside me on the sofa.

"That's right. And don't say *broad*."

"She sounds like a broad the way you've described her."

"Well, maybe she is. Anyhow, both weddings were called off and both would-be grooms were killed on the dates they'd planned to marry."

"And tell me again about the library."

I took a few sips of my drink before I started. "My theory was that if there was no real connection between the grooms, then there must be a serial killer on the loose."

"Ever think you watch too much TV, Sasha?"

"Shut up and let me finish. Dead fiancé one and dead fiancé two — I just had a hunch that if I went looking for it, I'd find other dead guys that fit the pattern. So I checked old newspapers for other guys whose 'I do' became an 'I don't.'"

"And?"

"Well, I would have seen it sooner if I hadn't just looked at it from a Christian point of view. And if I'd thought of Gordon as a middle part, not as the beginning."

"Huh?"

"A young single man, Bogdan Leonovich, was killed on Saturday, May 31, last year. Gordon was killed Saturday, July 5, and Jeffrey Keilor this year on Saturday, April 11. The other guy, Ryan Silverberg, was Jewish. Jews usually marry on Sundays. That's why it took me a while to notice him. Sunday, December 21. His death was reported in the Monday paper, not Sunday like the other ones."

"Holy shit!"

"Exactly. There are four dead guys, and I think the wedding planner killed them. Of course, I have no proof and I have no idea what her motive could have been."

"Are you sure she was involved in the other two weddings? Were those weddings called off, too?"

"No to the first and I don't know to the second. I found names in the obituaries for both of the ex-girlfriends or fiancées or whatever they were. Guess what I'll be doing tomorrow ..."

"You should take this to the police."

"You're right. I should. But I'm not going to. Not yet. I could still be wrong about a whole lot of things, and believe me, I still have a lot of questions about Darren, Christine, and Rebecca. I don't want to look like a fool or a conspiracy theorist or some little wet-behind-the-ears private eye. I'll go to the police when I'm sure."

"I think you're acting like a fool right now. Imagine if you'd been in your office when it got broken into?"

"I know, but I wasn't there, and I'm safe and sound."

"And stubborn," Mick said.

"I make my own decisions. I just want to find out from the other women if they used the same wedding planner."

Mick wisely didn't say anything more. He knew me well enough to know that once my mind was made up there was no changing it. I flipped on the TV, and we watched the news in silence.

# Sunday, April 19, 3:00 a.m.

When I woke up, I had a sore neck. Mick and I had both fallen asleep on the couch. We'd spent the rest of evening in mostly comfy silence, watching old black-and-white movies. I had no idea what time I'd drifted off. I tried to remember what movie we'd been watching and wondered if I'd seen the ending. Not a clue.

I went upstairs and got the comforter off the bed in the spare room and went back downstairs to tuck Mick in. Then I turned off the TV, which was now showing an infomercial for a piece of exercise equipment guaranteed to help you lose inches from your ass in no time at all or your money cheerfully refunded.

Going to my room, I curled up in bed and stared at the darkened ceiling. I tossed and turned for as long as I could stand it, then I gave up and went back downstairs. I checked the driveway on my way to the den and, sure enough, Shane's car wasn't there. I realized I would have been alone if Mick hadn't come over, and that made me shiver.

I went into the den and turned on the computer. The files I'd saved on the USB stick were still on this computer's hard drive. Just to be safe, I zapped an email to myself and sent all the files as an attachment. Even if this computer got trashed, too, I'd still have a cyber copy of the Hazelton and Harbourfront info.

Dad had sent another email with a brief update about his gambling excursion. He had taken Turning Stone Casino for as much as he could and then he'd swung northward from Albany. He'd headed to Upstate New York, really upstate, near a town called Massena, which was minutes from the Canadian border, and was now trying his luck at Akwesasne Resort and Casino. He said his latest shuffle-tracking theory, which made no sense to me, seemed profitable. He was now up more than four thousand dollars and planned to be home by midweek. I sent another cheeky reply about the pony I wanted for my birthday and gave him a very abbreviated, heavily edited update on my latest case. There was no point telling him about the office break-in.

I kept thinking about my office and who had been enough of an asshole to trash it and why. Darren seemed the most likely candidate. He was volatile enough to do something like that, and I had absolutely no reason to think that El Janitoro at his office hadn't blown the whistle on me. Of course, it could also have been

Christine, and there was no reason to think that Rebecca hadn't been involved. And then there was also the faint, remote, unlikely, highly improbable, but still possible, slim chance that it had just been a random burglary. Yeah, right. And Gordon had been a random victim, as had Jeffrey, Ryan, and Bogdan. Sure.

Around five in the morning I finally fell back asleep. Around seven I felt a hand on my face and awoke with a blood-curdling scream. "What the fuck are you doing in my room?" I hollered at Mick.

"You were having a nightmare. I could hear you all the way downstairs."

"I was? Oh, my God, yes, I was in an alley." I shivered.

"*Shh*. It's okay now. You let out one hell of a wail. I've been standing outside your door for the past five minutes. I didn't know if I should come in or if that would scare you even more. I didn't mean to startle you."

"God, I was up most of the night. Is there any chance either of us will get back to sleep?"

"Maybe if we were in the same bed …" Mick flashed me one of his million-dollar sheepish grins.

"Nice try, but not a chance. Let's go make some coffee."

After making the coffee, we sat in the kitchen and talked about the case.

"Okay, so here's what I want to find out," I told Mick. "I want to know about the girls the other two dead guys were seeing or not."

"You've said that already."

"So I'm saying it again. Sue me." Sleep deficit plus caffeine deficit equalled patience deficit.

"Okay ..."

"Sorry. I think I already know what I'm going to find out from them. If I confirm my suspicions, then I'm going to want to find out all I can about Valerie, the wedding planner."

"It's not even eight o'clock yet. You aren't going to get hold of anyone at this hour, especially on Sunday."

"Well, since we've got time to kill, do you want to help me clean up my office?"

"Do I have a choice?"

We grabbed a stack of green garbage bags and a roll of paper towels and were out the door. For the next two hours we tidied up as best we could, but most things were beyond redemption.

"I'm going to need a new computer and monitor," I said.

"What about the data stored on the hard drive? Please tell me you have copies."

"I do, thank God. I save everything onto a DVD or a USB flash drive and leave it with the Asian masseuse down the hall. She's the one with that Siamese cat."

"Is that safe? Can you trust her?"

"Absolutely. I don't stick my nose into her business, and she doesn't stick her nose into mine."

"Maybe if she'd stuck her nose in yesterday, your office would still be in one piece."

"Yeah, well, *if* is a pretty big word."

# *Sunday, 12:45 p.m.*

Anna Tambor had agreed to speak with me when she got home from church. I showed up as we had planned, but she seemed annoyed at my arrival. She showed me to a seat at the dining table in her small but nicely furnished apartment. I took the chair she indicated, but she remained standing. She didn't offer me coffee or tea, or even water.

"I don't know why you're asking about Bogdan. He's gone. Nothing will change that." Although her grammar was better than that of most native English speakers, her Slavic accent was still pretty thick when she spoke.

"I'm sorry if I'm opening old wounds. I'm a private investigator, and I think the case I'm working on right now has some similarities to what happened to Bogdan. Were you and he still a couple when he was killed?"

"No. We broke up a couple of months before. I found out he'd cheated on me with one of my co-workers. I don't like to speak ill of the dead, but he was a cheating bastard. I found out about their fling, dumped him, called off the wedding, and quit my job all in the same week."

"Man, what a crappy week."

"You have no idea. It was so bad, it didn't even seem real. Like it was happening to someone else."

"Did he stay with the other woman?"

"Hell, no. She was already married! Of course, that didn't work out, and Bogdan came slithering back to me, but I said no. Five or six weeks later he was a page two story in the *Toronto Sun*."

"Did the police suspect you?"

"Yes, but not for long. I was in Bratislava visiting my family when he was killed."

"Was the date of his death the same date as you'd planned for your wedding?"

"Yes. How did you know?"

"This might seem odd, but I need some details about your wedding plans." I handed her the same fill-in-the-blank page I'd given Angela and Christine.

"I hardly remember any of these details now. I think the banquet hall was called The Venetian or something like that. No idea about the DJ or the limo. The florist was the one in the Carson Grove mini-mall. I don't know the name, but it's the only flower shop there."

"Did you use a wedding planner?"

"Yes … Valerie something. Are you planning to get married?"

"No. At least not for a while."

"Fine. So if that's everything …"

*Here's your coat, what's your hurry? Don't let the door hit you on the way out.*

Shane was in the kitchen when I got home, and if you think that meant a gourmet meal was in the offing, think again. Something like "shoemaker's wives go barefoot" or "chef's sisters eat crap at home" applied. He created culinary masterpieces at the restaurant, but here he ate whatever came in a can, box, or microwavable package. I chose my own frozen entree, nuked it, and joined Shane for a delicious meal in minutes so I could have more quality time with my family. Or something like that. He almost fell off his chair when I gave him the latest update.

"Unbelievable. Your office was trashed?"

"Yup. There was a lot of damage, but Mick helped me clean it up. I just won't be able to work there till I get a new computer. And an alarm system."

We chatted a while longer and then I excused myself and went into the den so I could do some cyber sleuthing. I had less success finding Rachel Bluth than Anna Tambor. There were several listed in the phone book, but none was the right one. I really hoped she hadn't married someone else and changed her last name. I Googled her name and came up with a whole lot of hits for Rachel Bluths I wasn't interested in — some dead, some in Europe, two in Australia, and a few much too old to be the one I wanted.

Then I did a name search on Facebook and came up with six Rachel Bluths, all of whom looked about the right age, if their profile photos were current. In each case the detailed profile was blocked from anyone not listed as a friend, but I could email each of them, and that was exactly what I did six times.

To: Rachel Bluth
From: Sasha Jackson
Subject: Ryan Silverberg

Hello,

My name is Sasha Jackson, and I'm a private investigator in the Toronto area. I need to get in touch with the Rachel Bluth who was once engaged to Ryan Silverberg. Mr. Silverberg was killed on December 21, 2008. His murder has never been solved. I believe I have some information that would bring his case to a close, but I need to confirm a few details with his (former) fiancée.

Please contact me at this email address or at 416-555-1212.

Thank you,
Sasha Jackson

## *Sunday, 4:26 p.m.*

---

Queen's Quay Terminal was an upscale touristy shopping mall on Lake Ontario, and it was home to

Christine's Harbourfront gallery. If I hurried, I could make it to Queen's Quay Terminal by five o'clock, which would give me an hour of browsing before it closed at six.

I had no idea what it was, but something about my visit there yesterday was niggling at my brain. I was halfway tempted to call Victor and ask him to tag along, just for the entertainment value of seeing him interact with Christine. However, I didn't know if Christine would be at the gallery and didn't want to be stuck with him. And, yes, I realized those last few thoughts were selfish and unkind.

"May I help you?" asked a dapper young man when I entered the gallery. He was dressed too smartly to be working retail, even if the product was art.

"No thanks," I said. "Just looking."

The clerk nodded and silently walked away. I stuck my headphones in my ears and turned up the MP3 player. It was true that I was looking, but for facts, not artwork souvenirs, and I didn't want to be bothered while doing so.

I wandered around the gallery, gazing at various pieces but paying particular attention to the wall of paintings. The Inuit sculpture didn't merit more than a quick glance, but the aboriginal paintings and drawings were worth closer inspection. They reminded me of the ones I'd seen at Darren's office.

An American couple came in and peered at miniature carvings. They picked a small polar bear, not more than two by three inches, and paid over a hundred dollars for it. The dapper clerk took great care packaging the polar bear in non-recyclable bubble wrap, which I was sure actual polar bears appreciated very much.

I moved to the back wall to get a better look at some of the landscapes. My interest seemed to generate attention from the next group of tourists who walked in. They stood gawking at the painting of the mountain stream, and I shifted aside to let them gape en masse. Besides, I'd already seen what I'd come in for.

Now that my hunch had been mostly confirmed, I decided to call Victor, after all. I had a feeling I'd soon end up hating myself for it, though.

"Sure, I'm free," he told me over the phone, "and I'd love to meet up with you. In fact, why don't we have dinner? It's almost six o'clock, and I'm kind of hungry. What are you in the mood for? We can go anywhere you'd —"

"Well, I'm at Queen's Quay Terminal, so I'm flexible. Anywhere downtown."

"What a coincidence. I'm real close. I just saw the matinee at the Royal Alex Theatre."

"Wow, that's practically right next door to where I am," I said sarcastically. "How about somewhere on King Street West?"

"Okay, let's go for chicken wings at the Wheat Sheaf," he suggested.

"Perfect. I'll be there in twenty minutes."

The Wheat Sheaf was one of Toronto's oldest bars. It had been in operation since 1849, and if the walls could talk, I bet the stories would be unbelievable. I could only imagine who had passed through the doors during the past one hundred and sixty years.

Victor was seated at a table big enough for eight

people, right in the middle of the room, under a speaker blaring the latest hockey match.

"Maybe we should move to a table for two, Victor," I suggested. "What if a big group comes in?"

"You know, Sasha, you're right. I never thought of that. I sat here so I could keep my eye on the door and see you when you —"

"No problem. How about over there?"

The waitress brought menus and asked us for our drink order as soon as we relocated.

"Do you like draught beer?" Victor asked me. "I think beer goes best with chicken wings, and we can share a jug if you'd like, or if that's too much we can just order a couple of pints. Whatever you want to do is fine with me."

I could already see that this get-together had clearly been a bad idea, though I'd had my reasons for calling him. "We'll have a pitcher of Creemore, please," I said to the perky waitress.

"So what's up, Sasha?"

I waited, expecting him to run on for a few more sentences, but that was all he said. "Huh?" I finally blurted.

"You must have something on your mind, something about your latest case. It's just such a surprise, albeit a pleasant one, to hear from you out of the blue like this."

The jug of beer arrived, and I poured a couple of glasses. "Cheers," I said, and we clinked glasses. "Actually, I wanted to pick your brain about a few things."

"Sure. I'm happy to help. Fire away. Ask me anything."

"What was Christine's gallery like? The one at Hazelton Lanes."

"Huh? What was it like? Kind of small, but it seemed nice. Why?"

"What kinds of art did it have on display?"

"I don't know much about art. It was just a bunch of paintings."

"Were they landscapes? Expensive? Abstract? Oil paintings? Did you recognize any of the paintings or the artists?"

"Oh, I see what you mean. Well, it was all modern-looking. No pictures of anything that looked like anything I could figure out. You know, like most of the paintings were stripes and splashes and geometric shapes and stuff. Why?"

"I can't tell you right now, but I think, in a way, you've answered one question."

The basket of spicy wings arrived, and we were quiet while we munched on the pub grub. Victor managed to get wing sauce on his sleeve and on the tip of his nose. Without being asked, the waitress dropped off an extra stack of serviettes.

I'd now determined that Christine, Rebecca, and Darren were all bad guys, and I was pretty sure I knew how, even though I didn't understand a big chunk of their scheme. It didn't matter. Time would tell, and none of it had anything to do with the murder, anyway. The last piece to fit in was Ted. I hadn't yet followed up on Dad's advice to learn more about him. That was now priority number one. Actually, two. Finding Rachel Bluth was priority number one, but that was out of my hands for now, so by default Ted got promoted.

Having been the one who had suggested the get-together, there was no way I could now tell Victor I had a pressing prior engagement. So I resolved to enjoy the time out. Once you got past the nerdiness and the run-amok mouth, Victor was actually quite nice, and he was rather interesting and very intelligent.

"You've gone trekking in the Himalayas?" I said incredulously when he started telling me about a trip he'd taken.

"Yes, a couple of times, once just after university and again about four or five years ago. It's fascinating. If you ever get a chance, you should do it, though altitude sickness isn't very much fun."

Mountains, apparently, were his thing. He'd also been to the Alps, the Rockies, the Andes, even the Urals. This passion surprised me. I'd figured him to be the type who was afraid of heights.

We were ready to wrap things up at the Wheat Sheaf just before nine. We'd had a second basket of chicken wings and a second jug of beer. That, too, had surprised me, since I'd never seen him drink alcohol before. We were both a little bit tipsy, so we leaned against each other for support as we staggered outside and tried to hail two cabs. A little red light went on inside my brain as we stood there, and I stepped away from Victor and leaned against a lamppost instead. No matter how innocent and platonic, any kind of physical contact with Victor was a bad idea.

When I got home, I checked the answering machine.

Mick had called and left a message. Lindsey had called and left a message. Neither call was so important that it couldn't wait till tomorrow. There was a call for my dad, and I saved it without listening to it, though it probably wasn't particularly private. While I was at it, I also finally checked the voice mail on my cell. I had turned the ringer off when I got home last night and had forgotten to turn it back on. There was a message from Angela and another one from Ted. Both could wait till tomorrow. Last night's lack of sleep had finally caught up with me.

## Monday, April 20, 10:00 a.m.

"**I** need a fiancé for a few hours," I said into the phone. "Can you help me out?"

"What?" Not surprisingly, Mick sounded surprised.

"I have an appointment with Valerie the wedding planner, at two this afternoon. It's near Yonge and Eglinton. Can you come with me, please, please, please?"

Last night when Victor and I leaned against each other while waiting for our cabs, I'd fleetingly thought of asking him to play the role of my fiancé. I'd dismissed the idea almost as soon as it had come to me. I'd also thought of asking Ted and had called him this morning, but had gotten his voice mail once again.

Of course, I'd acted first and worried about the

details afterward. I'd already booked the appointment with Valerie and now needed an emergency groom.

Mick was the best choice. Or maybe he was my only choice.

"You're pretty sure she killed a bunch of guys and you want to go see her?" he asked me.

"Well, she only killed the ones whose engagements were called off."

"So, what, we'll really get married? Isn't that a bit extreme? Talk about going above and beyond for a client." Mick mostly sounded annoyed, but I think part of him was amused. At least I hoped so.

"I just want to get a sense of who she is and what she's like. As soon as I get one or two answers, I'm going to go to the police."

"Really?"

"Yes, really." I was kind of lying, but not exactly. I would go to the police eventually. When I was certain they wouldn't laugh at me.

"How long will it take? I have a job to finish by tomorrow." Mick was a freelance editor and worked from home. Like me, the haphazard musician's life had fostered in Mick a loathing of the nine-to-five routine. He had a flexible schedule, but always seemed to be rushing to meet deadlines.

"Probably an hour," I said. "Not more than that."

"Okay, I'll meet you there."

I gave him the address. "And remember, we're supposed to be engaged, so try not to act like a jerk."

That plan was now in action.

Next I returned Angela's call. She was curious about the investigation and was intrigued about my meeting with Anna Tambor.

"So you might really be onto something," she said.

"I think so. I hope so. I'll keep you posted."

That was supposed to have been my exit line, but Angela was feeling chatty, asked a few more questions, and offered lots of comments and ideas to each of my replies. I faked a coughing fit to get her off the phone.

Item three on my to-do list was checking email and Facebook. Three Rachel Bluths had replied. The first thought my email was an offensive joke, and she lambasted me online. The second was a generic but polite "Sorry, can't help you." The third said she lived in Vancouver and had never heard of Ryan Silverberg.

I hoped the other three would reply soon, though there was no guarantee I'd hear from them at all. Online communications were easy to ignore.

While I was in my hyper-proactive mode, I called Air Canada to find out when Rebecca's next trip was scheduled. May 10 to 11. I confirmed "my" seat assignment, and just for fun, made a request for a lactose- and gluten-free meal.

"We no longer offer meal service on flights of that duration."

"Oh. Well, can I bring my own food onto the plane?"

"New government restrictions limit the items passengers are permitted to bring into the cabin."

"So is that a yes or a no?"

"Food and beverage items are generally not allowed

once you've cleared security."

"So you won't give me a meal, but you make it almost impossible for me to bring my own food?"

"That's correct."

Next up was a call to one of my old professors at Sheridan College. I had a few questions that weren't covered in the textbooks. The program coordinator, Bryan Bessner, was glad to hear from me. I had been the teacher's pet, of course, and he was more than happy to help me out. I explained my current case and my theories and told him what I needed.

"I'll give my friend Petra Macpherson at Customs and Immigration a call. I'm sure she'll be interested in hearing this story."

After my last visit to Christine's gallery, and after my chat with Victor, I was pretty sure I'd figured out the art angle and how it connected with the Bahamas. "Thanks," I told Bryan. "Tell her to call me anytime day or night. Give her my home and cell numbers."

"Will do."

*Wow!* It was only 12:45, and I'd already rocked the world, or had at least set a lot of wheels in motion. I tried calling Belham again, but his secretary said he was out of the office. Damn it! I rang Lindsey just to touch base, but she could only give me a few seconds before she had to rush off to meet with a mortgage broker. With no one left to phone or email, I grabbed my jacket and headed to the subway.

I got to Yonge and Eglinton around 1:20, which was good. I needed some time to find a mock engagemen ring. There was a fashion-accessories store in the mall, and I hoped they'd have something in a cubic zirconia or a crystal that would do the job for now.

I was unsure how to dress for a wedding consultation. I'd left home wearing my black knee-high boots with black tights, a denim skirt, and a white cashmere sweater. Suddenly, I felt underdressed and impulsively bought a flashy red scarf and some earrings to jazz up the outfit. At the store next door I found a really funky black belt with a brushed enamel buckle, so I bought that, too. I was just about to walk out of the mall when I realized I had no ring. I ran back to the accessories shop and picked a "gold" banded ring with a "diamond" solitaire offset by several little "rubies" that matched my new red scarf. The ring cost $19.99, and I really hoped it didn't look it.

Mick was already in Valerie's frilly pastel office when I got there a few minutes after two. He greeted me with a great big sloppy wet kiss. I gently bit his tongue, and if he hadn't retreated, I was prepared to chomp down on it hard.

"Nice to meet you. I'm Valerie."

She looked like a young, rather buxom version of Queen Elizabeth but spoke with a nasal American twang. I halfway expected her to give me the Royal Wave with one hand while brandishing the Stars and Stripes in the other, but she gripped my hand in a firm shake instead. I noticed there was no jewellery on any of her fingers.

"Is that a Yankee accent I hear, Valerie?"

"Good ear. I'm from Syracuse, New York, but I've been here for a few years. My dad's Canadian."

"Well, how about that? So is mine."

I got a tight smile in response to that.

"A friend of mine gave you an excellent recommendation," I said.

"That's nice to hear. Whose wedding was it?"

"The wedding never actually happened. It was Christine Arvisais." I watched for a flicker of recognition and saw none. "Even though it was cancelled, she said you did an amazing job planning a dream wedding."

"Yes, well, you must both be so excited about this special time in your lives. Marriage is the biggest decision you'll ever make."

"We know it is," Mick said, obviously enjoying himself. "Sasha and I are deeply in love and we're more than ready to make the commitment."

I could see how the rest of the meeting was going to unfold. He clutched my hand and batted his eyes at me. If he was going to wind me up, he was going to have to take as good as he got.

"Yes," I said, "we're in love and we're so excited about starting our life together and our family. We want at least five or six kids." I could sense Mick having a minor coronary as soon as I said that. "We want it to be a really big wedding. It seems only fitting to start our life together with all our friends and family present."

"How many guests were you thinking of?" Valeri asked.

"At last count I figured there would be close to th hundred."

"Hmm," Valerie said. "That's fairly large, h

a good number to work with. I know of several ideal locations for a reception that size."

"So you handle all the planning?" Mick asked. "Dresses and menus and music and everything?" I knew he was about to sandbag me.

"Certainly. I offer full service, everything from engagements through honeymoons. Was there something special you had in mind?"

"Yes. I don't mind leaving most of the ceremony stuff to Sasha, but I have a few ideas about the reception I'd really like to see happen."

"Like what?"

"Well, it's a happy day and a celebration of love. I'd like some clowns to entertain the guests during the before-dinner cocktails. A lot of the guests will be bringing their kids, so maybe a clown who can juggle or make balloon animals?"

Clowns at my wedding? Other than the bride and groom, I'd have never thought of it.

"Well, that's certainly a creative idea. I'll look into it. Before we go any further, I need you to fill out these questionnaires. It's really just a profile sheet of your backgrounds, tastes, preferences, and interests. The better the background I have, the better I can tailor a wedding to suit you."

She handed each of us a four-page survey that covered ⸻rything from shoe sizes and favourite ice-cream flavours ⸻llergies and hobbies. And a lot more. On page one it ⸻ for occupation, and I couldn't think of anything ⸻so I wrote "art dealer." I figured that would explain my "friendship" with Christine should that question arise.

"Why do you want to know about hobbies?" I asked.

"That info's helpful in two ways — one for the bridal registry, and two, for ideas about themes for the reception or honeymoon."

"Oh."

"And allergies?" Mick asked.

"You'd be surprised how the big day can be ruined by a sneezing fit over flowers or an itchy rash from a woollen suit."

"I see."

We spent the next hour talking about our budget and our colour schemes and how many attendants we planned to have. Of course, we agreed on next to nothing. I wanted a church service; he wanted a civil ceremony. I wanted a sit-down dinner; he wanted a buffet. I hoped the gentle bickering gave our act a degree of verisimilitude.

"So what did that accomplish?" Mick asked as soon as we got out of there.

"A lot. I know she's American, which is certainly a useful detail. I know what she looks like, which is handy. I think I also know where and how she finds her victims. And I know she's not married, because there was no bling-bling on her left hand. Unlike my beautiful rock." I held up my left hand and could see that there was a pale green line around the ring band. "Cheapskate," I teased Mick.

"I'm saving money to buy booties for all those kids we're going to have." We both started laughing at the ridiculousness of it all. "I guess you now know that I'm passionate about clowns."

"Sure. A wedding wouldn't be complete without clowns, and maybe some jugglers, too. Of course, you know that means I won't budge on the Gregorian chants."

"You've got to be kidding. That's grounds for divorce."

We laughed some more as he walked me to the subway station.

"I'd give you a ride home, but I completely forgot to bring another helmet."

"Not to worry. Once we get married, your biker days are over."

# Monday, 6:03 p.m.

"Look, if you're not going to come in tonight, then don't bother coming back at all. We need reliable girls." Harvey, my boss at the smutty call centre, obviously cared more about profit than about my physical well-being.

"But I have a cold." I coughed a few times and said *hab* instead of *have*.

"I don't care. I have a business to run. Goodbye."

"But —" I was talking to the dial tone.

Damn it! That was the second time I'd been fired in as many weeks. Who got fired from a phone sex job, anyway? I didn't know whether to be mad about it or relieved. The paycheque was good, but the job description …

Obviously, I wasn't really sick. I just had a million things to do and wanted to do them all ASAP. I hadn't started any of them yet because I was fuming from the phone call. I went into the kitchen and made myself a sandwich, even though I wasn't hungry. I had taken one bite out of my ham and cheese on marble rye, still stewing over the firing, when my doorbell rang. God, I hoped it was a Jehovah's Witness. I was really in the mood to take my mood out on someone else. I peered through the peephole. Victor! Almost as bad as a messianic religious zealot. Time for a new job, new home, and new identity.

"Victor, what brings you here?" I made zero effort at disguising my bitchiness.

"I was in the neighbourhood and wanted to drop these off for you." He handed me a stack of photo albums.

I was still lodged in the doorway and made no move to invite him in.

"They're my photographs from my Himalayas trip. You seemed so interested in mountain trekking that I thought you'd like to see the photos. Maybe it'll give you some ideas about travelling, and I could sure help you plan a trip. I could even go with you if you —"

"That's nice, Victor, but this isn't a good time. Why don't you leave these with me and I'll look at them later?"

"Okay. But give me a call if you have any questions. Most of the prints are labelled with time and date and location, and I even wrote the names of whoever's in the photos. Of course, you won't know any of the people, so the names don't really —"

Was fate trying to tell me something? Like maybe I should take up recreational glue sniffing?

"Sure, I'll call if I have any questions. But I really have to go now. The kettle's whistling." I smiled at him as nicely as I could and backed inside the house. Powers of suggestion. I suddenly had a hankering for a cup of Earl Grey, so I put the kettle on.

Next up was a call to Ted. He and I had been playing phone tag for the past couple of days, and my talk with him was long overdue.

"Finally!" I said when he answered. "You're a hard one to reach."

"Sorry about that. I've been meaning to touch base with you, too. I'm kind of tied up for a while, but could we go for a drink around nine?"

"Sure. How about Myth on the Danforth? It's near Chester Avenue."

"I know the place. See you there then."

I should have been excited and giggly at the prospect of seeing him, but I wasn't. Maybe it was just general bitchiness after being fired and the surprise visit from Victor. Or maybe my head was clouded after seeing Mick again. Once again I started thinking about what married life with Mick would be like. I tried to picture our kids and wondered which of us they'd resemble. What? Did I even want kids? I figured they'd have my blond hair and his smile, and they'd definitely be musical. I'd encourage drums or piano, and Mick would be in favour of anything with strings. I then pictured us bickering over how to raise them and who would change diapers and who would do the laundry, and

I remembered why we were no longer a couple.

There was no way I'd ever get back together with Mick, but I had to admit it was fun pretending to plan a wedding with him. Once upon a time I'd thought that was what I really wanted. More than anything. And the kiss today. *Wow!* Sweet memories. Lusty memories.

I slapped myself upside the head and pictured the warning labels on household cleaners and paint thinners. TOXIC. COMBUSTIBLE. CORROSIVE. I pictured Mick with all those symbols tattooed on his forehead. I even thought of the warning HARMFUL IF SWALLOWED, but that almost made me want to call him.

Moving into the den, I logged onto the Internet. As comfy as the den at home was, I really missed my office. I hadn't been back to it since Mick and I had cleaned it up. I missed having my own workspace, but I wasn't sure I wanted to keep renting there. I just didn't like the feeling of working in a place someone had violated. I checked my email and was delighted to see more spam in my Hotmail account. I switched over to Facebook and saw that I had two new friend requests from people I'd scarcely known in high school. Delete. There were a few pointless blurbs on my Facebook wall, and some funny videos from YouTube.

*And an email from Rachel Bluth.*

Maybe this evening would turn out well, after all. Her message included a cell number and said she looked forward to talking to me. Probably not half as much as I wanted to talk with her.

"Hello, my name's Sasha Jackson. May I please speak with Rachel Bluth?"

"Speaking. Hi, how are you?" She was obviously on a cell, and there was a lot of background noise.

"Good, thanks. Did I catch you at a bad time?"

"Not really. I'm just driving home. Worked late tonight."

"I can call you later if you'd prefer. This might be a rather upsetting conversation. Not good if you're behind the wheel."

"I'm okay. So, like, what information do you have or do you want about Ryan?"

"You were engaged to him?"

"Yes, I was."

"Was the engagement called off?"

"Yeah … how did you know?"

"I can't tell you that right now. Who decided to cancel the wedding?"

"Kind of both of us. Well, mostly him, but I, like, thought it over and I agreed. Eventually. He said we were too young to get married. There was no need to rush. We're both twenty-three, and I guess that is kind of young."

"Can you tell me a bit about the plans you'd made for the wedding?" I didn't want to lead her or to put words in her mouth, so I kept it open-ended.

"Well, it was going to be a traditional Jewish wedding. Was supposed to be on December 21. A winter wedding. I had a white velvet dress."

"What other details can you tell me?"

"The dinner was going to be kosher, of course, and very upscale. It was five courses. There was supposed to be live entertainment. We'd hired a local band that could play a little bit of everything, you know, like old stuff and new stuff. Kind of Top Forties."

I knew all too well about bands playing wedding gigs. "Mony Mony," "Locomotion," "Unchained Melody," et cetera, et cetera, et cetera. Been there, done that, bought the T-shirt ... three sizes too small, then cut off the sleeves and cropped the bottom half so I could show off my midriff.

"Wow, sounds like you had a nice wedding planned. It must have been a lot of work to make all the arrangements."

"Well, it would've been, but we hired someone to take care of it all for us. Valerie's Wedding Planning. Valerie's the very best. She, like, thinks of everything."

"Yes, I've heard about her from some friends of mine, and they all say she's great. Sorry to switch topics so suddenly, but what about Ryan's murder? What can you tell me about that?"

She gave me the *Reader's Digest* version of it, most of which I already knew from the news stories on microfilm.

"He was killed on his way home from a weekend with the Canadian Forces. He was a corporal in the Air Reserve. He did that two weekends a month."

"Oh, really?"

"Yeah. Kind of cool, eh? Anyhow, it was like any other weekend. He took the subway to Finch and then walked home from there. That night he didn't make it home. I keep wishing he hadn't walked that night. Maybe if he'd, like, taken the bus or had someone come to pick him up, he'd still be alive, but he always walked home from the subway. He said the walk relaxed him."

"I'm so sorry." Seems I'd been saying that a lot lately. It sounded so hollow. I didn't mean it to, but what else can you say to someone you don't know and about some dead guy you'd never met?

After I wound up that call, I made a few more. God, I was spending so much time on the phone lately that maybe it was a good thing I no longer had a job in a call centre.

Angela Livingstone was polite when I called her. She seemed so eager to help and, once again, I was on the phone longer than I'd intended, listening to her ideas and suggestions. I grunted "Yeah" and "Uh-huh" every few minutes and started a game of Solitaire. She yammered on about a lot of stuff that didn't interest me, but eventually she confirmed the hunch I'd called her about.

Anna Tambor was very businesslike, so at least that call was blessedly short. She, too, confirmed my hunch.

I then called Mrs. Hanes and suggested a meeting with her, Rebecca, Christine, and *moi* at the Hanes Manse tomorrow at ten. The missus agreed to the proposed meeting and even offered to call the other two to extend the invitation.

Mission accomplished. Next on the list: paging Dad. I really hoped this wasn't one of those times when he was in "the zone" — having a hot streak at the tables. When gambling was going well, and Dad was on a roll, it could take forever for him to check messages or call anyone back. Just in case, after I beeped him, I sent him an email with all the questions I wanted to ask.

# *Monday, 8:44 p.m.*

I took a flying leap and made a wild guess at Valerie's motive: all the guys who had been killed had severed their engagements. I suspected she'd been engaged once and had been dumped, as well. Now I needed someone to do some fact-checking for me. Dad was that someone.

At a quarter to nine, just as I was about to run out the door to meet Ted, the phone rang.

"Hey, Dad, how much do you love me?"

"Let me guess. You're broke."

"Nope, well, actually —"

"Never mind. Nice try. What do you want?" As usual Dad got right to the point.

"Well, this is actually for your benefit. How would you like to extend the gambling trip a day or two?"

"I could probably suffer through a few extra days of cards. Why?"

"Feel like doing some research in Syracuse? It's not too far from Turning Stone Casino, right?"

"I guess, but I've been heading north, back to the border. I'd have to backtrack."

"Back to my original question. How much do you love me, Daddy?"

I gave him a quick version of my theory and of what

I knew about Valerie O'Connor. Dad was taking notes as we spoke, and he made me repeat several things so he could write them down. I told him that all the details were in an email I'd sent him, but he made me tell him again, anyway.

"That's right, Dad. From Syracuse, about thirty to thirty-five years old. Looks like Queen Elizabeth."

"Poor girl. That's not a compliment."

"I assume O'Connor is her maiden name. I have no idea about date of birth or high school. The best way to start would be the local library. Dig through the microfilm for the past ten years or so and look for social notices with her name. If she was engaged, I'll bet there was an announcement in the local paper. If you can find that, then we're laughing. If not, then we'll —"

"We?"

"Uh, okay, you'll have to do things the long way and look for young unmarried men who got murdered on a Saturday."

"Gee, the engagement notice sounds much easier."

"Thanks Pop. I owe you huge for this. I promise I'll be a good girl and clean my room and eat all of my veggies and —"

"That's enough, smartass. I'll call you tomorrow."

---

I was more than twenty minutes late for my meeting with Ted, and that really irritated me. I hate it when other people make me wait and I hate making other people wait for me.

"Hey, over here." Ted was at a comfy booth. Perfect. Easier to relax and talk.

"I'm really sorry I'm late. Believe me, that almost never happens."

"Don't worry about it. It gave me a chance to check the backlog of messages on my BlackBerry."

"Don't you mean your leash?"

"Yes, sometimes it feels like that. But when you work for yourself, you're on duty all the time. I guess you know what I mean."

"Sometimes, though in my line of work, it's handy to be incommunicado at times. I didn't know you worked for yourself. What do you do?"

"I'm a wine importer and exporter. I handle a lot of special vintages, private collections, that sort of thing."

"You're not drinking wine right now. Isn't that some kind of conflict of interest?"

He laughed. "Brandy. Don't tell my boss. Would you like one?"

"No thanks. I'll just have a cappuccino."

We chatted a while longer about who we were and what we did. It was nice to have a brief distraction from the case for a while and to just talk about other things, but eventually we circuitously steered the talk back to Gordon.

"Rebecca chose a really nice wine when we were at the Park Hyatt, a Pinot Grigio. I forget what it's called."

"Palmina Alisos. The Hyatt is one of my clients. I import that wine from a lovely little vineyard in

California. The Hyatt and Monsoon are the only places in Toronto where you can get it."

*Ding, ding ding* — we have a winner! Bells sounded in my mind, a light bulb illuminated over my head, and a chorus of "Eureka!" silently echoed in my brain. I could see a connection between Rebecca and Ted, and I now knew I couldn't trust him as far as I could throw him. What a shame. All that gorgeousness and no integrity. There was nothing less sexy than a liar. But he was still my employer, and I was certain he hadn't killed Gordon. And I was equally sure I wanted his cheque for my services to clear.

He told me a bit more about the vineyard, but I wasn't really listening. Another piece of the puzzle had just fallen into place.

"Well, it may be a lovely wine, but it stings when you get it in your eyes." I told him about my outing with Rebecca.

He politely listened and nodded now and then as I gave him the updates. "Aside from that, what else have you found out? Any leads yet?"

"Actually, yes. I know who killed him, but I can't say anything just yet. Knowing it and proving it are two different things."

"Will you be able to get the proof?"

"Ask me tomorrow. All I can tell you now was that the killer was someone who knew Gordon peripherally. It wasn't a friend, relative, business associate, or anything like that. You wouldn't recognize the name of the person if I said it to you right now."

"Wow, secrets and intrigue. Aren't you worried that he or she could get away? Or even worse, might kill someone else?"

"Yes and no. The killer has no idea I'm onto him or her. And Gordon wasn't the killer's only victim, but I can assure you that no one is in danger right now. In another day or two it'll be all wrapped up and I'll hand it over to the police."

"We need to inform Mrs. Hanes and the others."

"That's already booked for tomorrow morning."

"I'll stay tuned. It'll be a relief to finally have closure."

And it was a relief an hour later when I said good night to Ted. He offered me a ride home, and I accepted, even though I really didn't want to be that close to him, drop-dead gorgeous or not. It wasn't as if I was suddenly afraid of him; I had just come to the realization that he was a dirtbag. In fact, all four of them were — Rebecca, Darren, Christine, and Ted.

Ted had unwittingly given me the missing clue in the art fraud and funny money story. I'd figured out most of it earlier, but now I knew the final piece. I also surmised that Rebecca was the one who had broken into my office.

The other three, Ted, Christine, and Darren, all had the same stories to hide, but conveniently were also one another's character witness or alibi or whatever. As long as one kept his mouth shut and covered for the others, they'd all be okay.

Rebecca was lumped into the same bullshit as the rest of them, but she was the only one with extra secrets to hide. The pills were one thing she wanted kept hush-hush and Ephraim was the other. She simply had more at stake than the rest, or thought she did. I was determined that tomorrow, somehow, I'd get her to voluntarily spill the beans about the boy when we all met at Mrs. Hanes's house.

## Tuesday, April 21, 9:40 a.m.

I got to the Hanes house a little bit early. I had another hunch I needed to confirm. "Do you have a copy of Gordon's will?" I asked Mrs. Hanes.

"Of course. Why?"

"Don't ask. May I have a look at it?'

She excused herself and came back a moment later with official-looking, legal-sized pages. "Here you go."

As soon as I skimmed through the document, I saw by absence the very thing I was looking for.

Soon after, Rebecca, Christine, Mrs. Hanes, and I were all sitting in awkward silence in Mrs. Hanes's beige living room, drinking incredibly weak tea and waiting for someone to break the ice. Rebecca looked as if she'd been crying, though maybe she was just stoned.

Christine, on the other hand, was dressed in a stern business suit. Judging by the expression on her face, she'd just spotted a cockroach scurrying under the table. "Will this take long? I simply must get to the gallery. I can't just drop everything."

I ignored her. "There are a number of things we need to air. You might not like some of what you hear, but I really don't care. Deal with it. Here goes."

Rebecca appeared worried while Christine stared impatiently. Mrs. Hanes concentrated on removing imaginary specks of lint from the sofa.

"For the record, you all knew Gordon was a good guy, and you all loved him very much. None of you would have hurt him in any way."

Christine snorted. "Of course not."

"I loved him like a brother," Rebecca said.

I continued. "This sounds crass, but a number of people were better off having Gordon alive than dead. He was very generous, right, Christine?"

"Yes."

"Mrs. Hanes knows he was helping you out. Fill Rebecca in on that story."

So Christine did, but grudgingly. I had to prompt her several times, and with each nudge, I got a "Fuck off" glare. *Humph, same to you,* I thought.

"He gave me money. Kind of like alimony, except we weren't divorced. He knew my mother and I had hit some financial snags —"

"At the casino?" Rebecca couldn't resist a chance to be catty.

"Please don't interrupt her," I said. "This all ties together."

"He wanted me and my mother to get back on our feet. He basically reimbursed me for all the wedding expenses. He said he'd help us turn the gallery into a viable business so that we'd eventually be financially independent." She revealed a few more details, most of which I'd already filled in myself. "Mom and I have been trying to avoid going into bankruptcy."

Rebecca seemed to take pleasure in hearing about Christine's financial struggles. Mrs. Hanes, on the other hand, hadn't said a word. I decided it was now time to pull Rebecca down a peg or two.

"Rebecca, Gordon trusted you more than anyone, didn't he?" I asked.

"Yes, of course. We confided in each other many times."

"Did he know about your drug addiction?"

"Pardon?" Mrs. Hanes finally spoke.

"What?" Christine said.

"Pill addiction? What are you talking about?" Rebecca's voice didn't carry enough conviction to fool anyone.

Christine tried unsuccessfully to mask a sneer, and Mrs. Hanes got busy picking at imaginary specks of lint. I was more than halfway tempted to rip open one of the feather-filled accent cushions and pitch its contents all over the place so Mrs. Hanes would have a reason to justify her nervous habit.

"Gordon trusted you, but not with money," I continued. "That's why the money he left you was in a trust account. He had a colleague named Snider keep an eye on the money."

"What are you talking about?" Mrs. Hanes asked.

"Who's Snider?" Christine demanded.

"It's probably better, Rebecca, if they hear it all from you," I said.

So she told them everything — about popping pills and duplicate prescriptions, about the four kinds of pills I'd found in her bag, plus a couple of others.

"It's an illness, dear," Mrs. Hanes said. "We can get you into treatment. There's no need to be ashamed."

"There's more to the story, right. Rebecca? Or would you rather they hear it from me?"

"I don't have a choice, do I?" Rebecca said.

"Nope."

She started with the climax and worked her way backward. No one interrupted her until she finished the whole tale. She mentioned spring break, golfing, and a one-night stand with a cocktail waitress at a resort. She gave them all the details about the court battles and the father-and son reunion.

"I have a grandson?" Mrs. Hanes said quietly. "He's eleven? Does he look like Gordon? What's he like?"

Christine was dumbfounded. "I never knew ... how could he have kept that from me?"

Mrs. Hanes was clearly overjoyed to learn that her son lived on through his son. She bombarded Rebecca with questions, while Christine sat in a snit, wondering when attention would finally shift to her.

"Okay, that's all the personal stuff out of the way," I said. "Now about the murder ..." I knew I was being abrupt and heavy-handed, but I wanted to get this wrapped up. I still had other things to do today.

"Yes, what did you find out?" Christine asked.

"Have you solved it yet?" Mrs. Hanes chipped in.

Rebecca was quiet; she'd done enough talking for one day. Christine looked as if she was trying to figure out how to work any and all of this meeting to her advantage. Good luck with that, bitch.

"Yes and no," I said. "I can't give you the killer's name just yet, but I will in another day or two."

"Why did he do it?" Rebecca asked.

"Who said the killer was a he?" Christine interjected.

"I think you should let Sasha tell us in her own way," Mrs. Hanes suggested.

I waited a moment before beginning my monologue. "Well, it wasn't a case of wrong time, wrong place. The killer knew Gordon, though not very well. I thought all along there was a connection to the wedding, and I kept looking at it that way until I figured it out. That's why I asked so many questions about the wedding plans."

Rebecca frowned. "One of the guests? A relative?"

"Should we be afraid?" Christine asked. "Are we still safe with a killer out there? What if he ... or she ... comes after us?"

"I don't think you have anything to worry about. The killer was only tangentially acquainted with Gordon. You needn't worry. It's not someone any of you are in contact with. And the killer doesn't know what I know."

"Well, if the killer only knew my son slightly, then why kill him?" Mrs. Hanes asked. "What could be the motive?"

"Sort of a combination of jealousy and a twisted sense of revenge. The killer knew that Gordon jogged every Saturday and waited for him. It was premeditated. That's all I can say for now."

# Tuesday, 11:30 a.m.

When I got home from my meeting with the bluebloods, Shane was just getting up after working until two. With a bad case of bed head and a stubbly chin, he suggested we go for breakfast at our neighbourhood greasy spoon. I wasn't very hungry but joined him, anyway. The only thing on my mind now was a call or an email from Dad. Realistically, I shouldn't have expected to hear from him till four or five o'clock in the afternoon at the earliest, but hope was the confusion that resulted from the conflict between desire for a thing and its probability.

Shane and I had a good talk over bacon and eggs. We hadn't had much one-on-one time recently, since we'd both been working erratic hours. Shane ate while I chatted and pushed the food around on my plate but hardly touched it. He dipped his toast in the egg yolks, and I tried not to gag. Something about the texture of a runny yolk made me think of soft little fuzzy yellow baby chicks. The waitress came by and refilled my coffee a third time.

"I guess if Lindsey and I ever decide to tie the knot, we'll elope," Shane said after I brought him up-to-date.

"Smart move. Any idea when that day will come?"

"It wouldn't be fair if I told you before I asked her. Hopefully soon. Hey, if you're not going to eat that bacon ..."

I pushed my plate toward him.

---

After such a late breakfast, I was absolutely beside myself with skittishness and anxiety. I knew I wouldn't be able to concentrate on anything, so I did something I'd been happily neglecting for the past month. I went to the gym and worked up a sweat. I did everything — weights, rowing machine, stair climber. After getting my heart rate up and pushing myself into the fat-burning zone, I dropped into a Pilates class and did my best to mirror the instructor. I hated working out, which was why I cheerfully accepted any excuse to skip it. The only thing that made it somewhat less horrible today was that I had my MP3 on, and it almost entertained me enough to forget momentarily that I was at a gym.

At three o'clock I went home and began my silent vigil. I sat at the computer, with the cordless home phone in front of me, my cell phone beside it, and my Hotmail, Yahoo, and Facebook accounts all open. No messages. I sat and waited. And waited.

At four o'clock I jumped out of my skin. I got a call from Petra Macpherson, the customs agent Bryan Bessner had referred me to. She was more than a little intrigued at the story I spun for her, even though for now I omitted names and spoke of it as a hypothetical situation. I told her how I imagined it playing out, and she was onboard with my idea, pending confirmation of some of the details.

"Let me wrap up another case and then we'll talk," I said. "We definitely have time before the next transaction." With a little planning and a little teamwork we'd be able to pinch the Silver Spoons for their art fraud/money laundering scheme.

At four-thirty I got a call from Mick, asking me what kind of flowers I'd choose for my bridal bouquet.

"Dandelions," I said.

"Very funny. If you keep that up, I'm going to insist on a prenuptial agreement."

At five o'clock I got a call form Valerie, inviting me to see some sample menus for three hundred wedding guests. "I thought we'd do buffet-style for appetizers and hors d'oeuvres. We can put out a nice spread during the cocktail hour. Afterward, we can do a seated three-course dinner."

"That sounds fantastic."

"I think it's a good way to compromise. And I have some ideas I'd like to show you for centrepieces. Would you care to come to the office this evening and have a look?"

"Tonight's not really good. I'm kind of busy right now."

"You don't have to come immediately. I'll be in the office till about eight o'clock. I have to catch up on some paperwork. Then I have to go see a client. Give me a call anytime before then if you want to drop by."

"Will do, but it's probably best if I wait till Mick's available to come with me. I don't think it's a good idea for me to make any executive decisions."

At 5:15 Lindsey called.

"Darling, I'd love to chat, but I want to keep the phone free. I'm waiting for a call from my dad."

"Sure, no problem," Lindsey said. "Is everything okay, though? I'm worried about you and this case."

"You're a good friend, Lindsey. I just hope you'll be there for me if I ever need someone to bail me out of jail."

At seven o'clock I got the anticipated call from Dad. "The wedding announcement was on September 22, 1997. Valerie O'Connor and Eric Quinty proudly announce their intention to marry, yadda yadda yadda …"

I whistled. "So I was right. She was once engaged."

"You were right about more than that. I figured I'd go the extra mile for my favourite daughter —"

"I'm your only daughter."

"Don't quibble over details. Eric Quinty's obituary was in a March 1998 newspaper."

"I don't suppose he died of natural causes?"

"No. Shot, random crime, wrong place, wrong time. Just like you thought."

"Shit. It's kind of scary that I was so right."

"You should go to the police now. You've gone far enough with this."

"I will," I lied. I'm pretty sure Dad didn't believe me, so I ended the conversation rather abruptly.

# Tuesday, 10:30 p.m.

The whole office break-in theme was getting a little worn out. First my visit to Darren's place of business, then Rebecca's violation of my corporate HQ. And now, for my latest caper ... Valerie's office.

I tried to tell myself that two wrongs do make a right and right a wrong, but I got confused by the whole convoluted adage. It didn't matter. I had the moral conviction that it was okay to do the wrong thing as long as it was for the right reason. Solving a serial murder and maybe preventing another death seemed to justify my actions.

I'd been planning this since before the fake wedding consultation yesterday. In fact, yesterday's appointment had primarily been to get some info about the wedding planner, which admittedly had been useful. However, my hidden agenda was to scope out her office so I could later pursue this nefarious nocturnal no-no. I wanted a peek at her files, just the ones for weddings that had been cancelled. I planned to go to the police tomorrow, and I had to be able to hand them the whole package, sans loose ends.

Valerie's office was on the second floor of a renovated four-storey heritage building that had once been a shoe warehouse. The original stone facade of the revamped structure had been maintained. Inside, the architects had opted to celebrate the features of the building's age and had removed the perforated pressed-board ceiling tiles to expose old pipes and beams that had now been painted matte silver. The door frames and baseboards were all made of salvaged distressed wood, and the lobby and stairwell were exposed brick. I was surprised that developers hadn't pushed for residential zoning to transform the building into funky million-dollar lofts.

Valerie's office door took a lot more work than I'd expected, but I wasn't worried. I'd noticed yesterday that there was no alarm. I jiggled at the doorknob several times, trying one tool after another. A clicking sound and then another jiggle, and I was in.

Her filing cabinets were as well organized as one would expect from a woman whose reputation was built on her attention to details. The top drawer contained current files and weddings for the next two years. Who planned that far ahead? Within each year the files were organized alphabetically, according to the bride's surname.

The second drawer was for completed files and again was divided into years — 2009, 2008, 2007, and 2006. These, too, were subdivided by the bride's maiden name.

The third drawer contained files that Valerie had labelled ON HOLD, and I got butterflies in my tummy. They only lasted for a second, though. These seemed to be files where there were conflicts with dates, mostly for weddings on waiting lists for a particular banquet hall. The Distillery and Enoch Turner Schoolhouse seemed to be in great demand; a number of couples were hoping a cancellation would open up availability for them. A few on-hold folders were for wedding plans with dates not yet determined. I wondered how much planning one could do if the bride and groom had no clue when their special date would be.

The bottom drawer had tons of brochures for suppliers: florists, caterers, and the usual suspects. They were useless for my purposes, though I did see some interesting buffet menus.

The second filing cabinet was a two-drawer model, and neither drawer had anything of interest to me. Expenses, blank contracts, the questionnaire Mick and I had filled out, accounts receivable, write-offs, and accounts payable. Boring.

I began digging through the on-hold files and saw nothing to indicate that any had been cancelled. I figured it would have been too easy to have it land in my lap like that. I glanced back at 2008 and discovered the closed files for Christine, Anna, and Rachel. Then I found the Angela Livingstone file in the 2009 — Closed section.

"Are you wondering who my next victim will be?" Valerie was standing in the doorway.

"What? Yes, no, huh? Fuck, I mean ... I was just ..." When I noticed the gun pointed at me, I reflexively contracted the muscles in my pelvic area to keep from peeing my pants.

"Just looking to see who else was on my hit list?"

"I came to see the menus ..."

Was that a real gun? It couldn't be. This was a joke. It wasn't loaded, was it? She wouldn't shoot me. She was bluffing.

"Bullshit," Valerie said. "There are two guys I've

got my sights on. Take a look at the other cabinet under write-offs."

I couldn't move. I couldn't breathe. The gun was pointed right at me. It looked real. Scarily real. Cold. Final. Deliberate.

"How did you find me here? How did you know?" My voice was a squeaky, cracking sound I'd never heard before. *Jesus Christ, get me out of here!*

"I've been sitting in the McDonald's across the street for the past hour and a half. I knew you'd come. That's why I phoned you. I wanted to make sure you knew when I *wouldn't* be here."

"How did you know I was onto you?"

"You're such an idiot. I recognized you and Mick, and I didn't fall for that bullshit lovey-dovey crap. I've been doing this for years, and there was nothing convincing about you two as a couple, especially your tacky drugstore ring."

"What do you mean you recognized us?"

A wave of fear washed over me, bigger than the one that had already enveloped me. It was a horrible feeling, more consuming than any emotion I'd ever experienced.

"Your band played at a couple of weddings I arranged."

"We did? How come I never met you?"

I tried to keep my eyes on the gun, but I couldn't look at it. I tried to keep my eyes on her and couldn't. I just wanted to explode, scream, run, hide …

The kaleidoscope of half-formed thoughts that whirled through my mind all led to dead ends, literally. I could try to hurl a stapler at her. Attempt to club her over the head with her Rolodex. Create a distraction and run for my life.

And I knew I'd be dead before I knew it.

"The bride and groom paid the band directly, so you never got a cheque from me. I made the bookings with your agent. I go to each of the weddings I plan, but I try to stay in the background and I usually leave once the party's in full swing."

*Oh, God, what about Mick?* "How did you know I was on to you?"

"You're so naive. You should've stuck with singing. You're quite good. I knew you were onto me when you mentioned Christine Arvisais. A jilted bride would never give a referral. Besides, you weren't on Christine's wedding invitation list."

She seemed absolutely calm, and that freaked me right out. I couldn't believe what was happening. It was so surreal. It almost seemed funny, kind of like one of those urban legends friends told around a campfire.

"You're going to shoot me, aren't you?"

"With a smile."

*Keep her talking. Think of something. Buy some time.*

"Humour me before I meet my maker. Why did you do it? Revenge on the clients who got cold feet? Spurned lovers who didn't pay the bills? Or are cancellations just simply bad for business?"

Both her hands were now holding the gun, and she seemed perfectly steady. I was standing about six feet from her and was about six seconds away from being six feet under.

"You're such an idiot," she said.

*Perform. Fake it. Don't show fear. The best defence is a good offence.*

"Let me guess. Eric Quinty dumped you, and now you're bitter."

Her eyes flashed at the mention of his name. My imitation bravado was gaining momentum.

"What did he do, dump you because you're a lousy fucking lay?"

I was either going to live through this or I wasn't. Either way, whatever I said now mattered little. So, I snapped. I didn't know if it was a conscious decision or not, but I completely lost it.

"Couldn't please your man, so he bailed? Or maybe he just realized he didn't want to spend the rest of his life married to a fucking cow."

I was screaming now. The gun was still pointed right at my chest. Her eyes squinted, and it looked as if she was ready to pull the trigger.

*Go out with a bang, Sasha. Go out with a bang.*

"Let me guess. You had your poor little heart broken and never got over the humiliation of being dumped."

"Shut the hell up! You have no idea what you're talking about." Valerie's voice was tight and creaky, but her hands remained steady on the gun.

"Maybe Eric found someone prettier than you or smarter or more fun. Maybe he realized he was the only guy dumb enough to want to marry you. But then he called it off. So you killed him, didn't you? You're so fucking pathetic. No wonder Eric didn't want you."

I'd pushed the right button. She finally reacted, loudly, shrilly, her icy composure melting away.

"It wasn't me! There was nothing wrong with me!" Her voice was at a pitch even dogs could hear. "Eric fucking decided he was gay. He was gay, and that's why he ended it, bitch. It wasn't my fault!"

I was seeing red. So was Valerie. I saw her trigger finger twitch. I saw my whole life flash before my eyes. I saw Victor holding a gun. The last thing I remembered was that gunfire in real life sounded a lot worse than on TV.

## Friday, April 24, 10:30 a.m.

"Can someone please get me a real coffee? This stuff is awful." I pushed aside the Styrofoam cup of crappy institutional fake coffee. I knew I was in pain, but I didn't know what the hell had happened, so I decided to complain about something tangible instead.

"Sure thing, princess," Dad said, pulling back the curtain. "Victor, would you like one, too?"

"No thanks," Victor mumbled in a sleepy, drugged voice.

"He's still pretty groggy," Lindsey said.

"So what the hell happened to him?" I asked. "To me? What are you all doing here?"

I was at Sunnybrook Hospital in a semi-private

room, with Victor as my bunk buddy. Dad was on his way out the door to get me something drinkable. Shane and Lindsey were standing at the foot of my bed. I didn't know why I noticed it now, but side by side their physical differences stood out. Shane, like me, had inherited genes from our father's side — blond and lanky. Lindsey at five foot two was a full twelve inches shorter than him and voluptuous. They made me think of a greyhound and a Pomeranian. Mick, looking just like the bad boy my dad had warned me about, was sprawled in the maroon vinyl chair by the window. I decided if Mick were a dog, too, then he'd be an Irish setter. I must have been loaded on painkillers. I liked dogs well enough, but had never had one, because Dad was allergic to them. Why was I even thinking of them now?

"What's the last thing you remember?" Lindsey asked.

"I was in that psycho bitch Valerie's office last night."

"It wasn't last night," Mick said. "It was Tuesday. Today's Friday."

"What the hell? I went to her office to go through her files. It was a setup. When I got there, she showed up and pulled a gun on me. Then Victor came in with a gun. And now I'm here. Did Valerie get away?"

"Valerie's dead," Mick said. "Victor shot her, but only after accidentally shooting you in the stomach. She fired at him, and he took two bullets."

"Holy crap! What the hell happened?"

Shane chuckled. "You don't remember? You were shot twice, too. Once by Victor. We're sure he's sorry about it and ... well, Valerie fired at you. Let's just say it could've been a lot worse. Thank God for the Kevlar cups."

"Huh?"

"You were lucky," Mick said.

"I don't feel very lucky right now. What happened?"

Lindsey laughed. "Your bra saved you. The second bullet probably would've gone into your heart if the underwire in your bra hadn't deflected it."

"You must be joking." I started to laugh, but a sharp pain zinged through my chest.

Shane grinned. "Nah, we've all been making up jokes about bras that lift and separate, eighteen-hour, .38 calibre support bras, cross your heart and protect it —"

"Padded," Mick said. "Don't forget padded."

"I don't wear padded bras. It was a push-up bra. The underwire saved me? Really?"

"Yeah, a few millimetres away and we wouldn't be having this conversation."

God, no wonder I was in hellish pain. "And what about Victor?"

"He was in critical care for a while," Mick said. "One of the bullets punctured his lung. It was touch and go at first, but he's been stable since yesterday afternoon."

"How did we end up in the same room?"

"Oh, we asked them to put you together. We told the ward nurse that he's your boyfriend. You know, in some cultures if someone saves your life, you become their servant."

"Bite me, Mick. So Valerie's dead?"

"Victor saved your ass and got rid of a psycho at the same time," Shane said. "He got really lucky after his practice round on you. Bang. One shot in the temple when she turned to fire at your boobs, and Valerie was DOA. Someone heard the shots and called 911."

"Holy crap."

"The police had a lot of questions," Shane said. "Dad, Lindsey, Mick, and I filled them in. Valerie's gun matched the gun used in the murder of all four guys."

"Has anyone spoken to the families?" I asked. "Mrs. Hanes and Christine? What about the others — Rachel, Anna, and Angela? Do they know what happened?"

"Everyone knows," Shane said. "The story's been all over the papers for the past two days. Here, have a look."

The three of them were snickering as Lindsey handed me the *Toronto Sun*. There was an eight-by-ten colour photo of my pink satin and lace bra on the front page under the headline: BRA SAVES WOMAN'S LIFE. SPURNED SERIAL KILLER SHOOTS SLEUTH'S UNDERWIRE.

"Now the whole city knows you're a 36-C." Mick could hardly contain his laughter. "Over-the-Shoulder Boulder Holder and Bullet Stopper."

"Or how about Two-for-One Double-Barrelled Slingshot and Shield," Shane said.

"We're thinking of having it bronzed." Lindsey was almost doubled over with laughter.

"I hate you. All of you."

Dad came back with a Grande Frappuccino with extra caramel and lots of whipped cream. I didn't know whether to drink it or throw it at the bunch of them. Whipped cream was dribbling down the edge of the cup, and I licked it up. Nothing had ever tasted so damn good.

"When will I get out of here?" I asked.

"Probably in a couple of days," Dad said. "You lost a lot of blood. A bullet in the belly will do that, you know. You had us all really worried."

That afternoon, and all the next day, our hospital room felt like Grand Central Station. Friends and relatives came to visit Victor and me one after another. Victor's mother brought homemade oatmeal cookies and sat with his hand in hers while he slept. Someone else gave us a big bouquet of balloons. We both got lots of colourful flowers and get-well-soon cards. At one point the floor nurse said the room was too crowded and asked visitors to come in pairs, while the others waited in the lobby. The noise was too distracting for Victor.

Later in the day Mrs. Hanes and Rebecca visited me. Mrs. Hanes smiled. "I can't tell you how relieved I am. Thank you."

"Now you can have peace," I said. "Nothing will bring him back, but at least you know."

"I'm going to focus on the positive. I have a grandson now, and I can't wait to meet him. I've talked to him on the phone, and I invited him to Toronto when school ends."

I noticed that the missus was wearing a splashy pink-and-magenta-flowered blouse, and her blue eyes had a sparkle I'd never seen before.

"My aunt refuses to fly," Rebecca said.

"I'm too old to be gallivanting all over the place, and I'm afraid of heights. Besides, don't you think Ephraim will enjoy visiting Toronto? Think of all the fun we can have showing him around. Wonderland, Ontario Place, Niagara Falls, the Science Centre."

"And the CN Tower," I said. "Don't forget that."

"I'll bow out of that excursion. Rebecca, you can take him there."

Angela was the next visitor, followed by Ted and Darren and then Rachel. Christine didn't visit me, but that was no surprise. However, I was amazed that Mr. Belham did.

"It's so nice of you to have come," I said to him.

"I read the story in the paper and thought it might have something to do with the questions you were asking me. It's clear who killed Gordon Hanes, and that it was a bizarre revenge killing. But I'm still curious about the other angles we spoke of, the Bahamas and offshore banking."

"Yes, sir, that, well … I stumbled onto the Bahamas case while I was investigating Gordon's death. I thought at first that they were connected, but they're two completely separate things."

"Well, how about that? Were you able to get resolution in the other situation?"

"Actually, not really. Not yet, anyway. That's why I was trying to phone you."

"Yes. My secretary told me you called more than once. So what would you like to know?"

I gave Belham an edited version of the conversation I'd had with Petra from Customs and Immigration. Belham was almost as impressed by the intricacies of the scheme as he was by my deductions.

# *Friday, May 8, 11:15 a.m.*

Victor had offered to accompany me as I checked out potential new office space. I would have preferred Lindsey as a tagalong, but she only did residential real estate. Other than our stay together at Sunnybrook, Victor and I hadn't seen much of each other since the shooting. He'd been injured much more gravely than I and would take a lot longer to fully heal. Today was his first outing, aside from appointments with his doctor, since being released from the hospital.

I'd made the decision to break the lease at my old office, but I was having a tough time finding something in the same price range that wasn't next door to a meth lab. I'd seen some nice offices that were way out of my price range. Too bad. Maybe in a few years when I expanded to Sasha Jackson and Associates, but not yet. For now I just wanted a place in a reasonably secure and clean building.

The agent showing us this latest place was a hardcore salesperson. Her forced enthusiasm was annoying, and I thought the muscles in her face would get sore from the perma-grin. It was as if she were pulling out every customer service trick she'd learned from her real-estate agent's sales training guide.

"The lease includes utilities and one parking spot in

246 *Jill Edmondson*

the underground garage. The building has central air, so you'll be comfortable in summer. The carpets were just steam-cleaned, and the office has been freshly painted, so you can move in right away." She gestured toward the walls and floors like one of the blond bimbos showing prizes on a TV game show.

It was a nice office, but I didn't want to commit yet. I had a lot to think about in terms of my professional life. I'd never before thought of investigating as dangerous. I'd always seen it as intelligence gathering and research, not violence. More like brains over brawn. Or bullets.

"I'm not sure. Victor, what do you think?"

He shrugged. "It's okay."

I had no idea why or how, but the shooting seemed to have affected Victor's mouth. When I found out that we were roommates in the hospital, my first thought had been that he'd talk my ear off so much that I'd want to shoot him, too. But right from the get-go he'd seemed different, quieter, not antisocial or uncommunicative, just whatever the opposite of long-winded is. Unverbose? Unloquacious? Unpalaverous? Unebullient? Unwindbag?

I glanced at the view from the office window. There was an uninterrupted panorama of a parking lot, the Gardiner Expressway, and the railway tracks. Charming. "What are the terms of the lease?"

The agent consulted her notes. "The landlord will rent it on a month-to-month basis. First and last month's rent deposit required. Thirty days' notice to terminate. No pets allowed in the building, except seeing-eye dogs, of course."

"Let me think it over for a day or two." I turned to Victor. "How about grabbing some lunch?"

"Sure. Something light. Maybe soup."

It was 12:20 now, and we were just a short walk from the St. Lawrence Market.

"If I took that office, I could have lunch here all the time. The neighbourhood is certainly a plus. It's very lively."

"It's nice."

I couldn't believe I'd ever think this, but I wished the old mile-a-minute-motor-mouth Victor would return. The taciturn guy he'd become wasn't nearly as amusing as the former chatterbox.

We got our homemade cream of broccoli soups and took our tray to a table outside.

"There's something I've been wondering about, Victor."

"What's that?"

"How did you know where to find me that night? How come you showed up?"

"Uh …"

"I'm not going to like this answer, am I?"

It was something I'd been wondering about for a while.

"Well …" He avoided answering by spooning a mouthful of soup.

"Were you following me?"

"Kind of …"

"You'd been following me for a while, hadn't you? Why? You aren't still hoping that you and I will ever —"

"It's not like that." His face reddened, and he glanced down at the table.

"You'd better explain, because the things I'm imagining are probably worse than the real story. You kept turning up too often for it to be a coincidence — at my office, at the museum."

"I was testing one of my inventions on you."

"What?"

"Please don't be mad. I was working on something. I wanted to test it, and you were a good choice."

"What the hell are you talking about?"

"There are so many electronic gadgets on the markets these days, but so many instruments are single-purpose. I wanted to try to combine two."

"Huh?"

"I was working on a hybrid global positioning device and MP3 player."

"You mean the one you gave me?"

"Yes."

"I can't believe you'd violate me like that. It's so invasive."

"It wasn't like that. I needed to test it on someone who had unpredictable patterns. I needed to check the accuracy and the range."

"So while I was listening to music, you were tracking me?"

"Usually. Sometimes the signal got jumbled. The music caused a lot of interference, especially when you were listening to Ozzy Osbourne."

"Gee, maybe I should've played it backward," I said.

"Or walked backward."

"I'd just worked out a bug in the programming and I was going to tell you, but I wanted to apply for a patent first. I'm calling it the Sasha Station."

*Wow!* No one had ever used my name for a patent before. Of course, I'd never been shot before or saved by an underwire bra before, so this was a period of growth and discovery in my life. Yeah, right.

"So, Victor, how did you know to bring a gun?"

"Well, I'd been following right behind you on the whole investigation. I knew what you were up to and figured it out about the same time as you did. You'd been home all afternoon and evening. When you went out at ten that night, I had a really bad feeling."

"I should be madder than hell at you, but I'm so damn glad you showed up. You saved my life."

---

It was three o'clock and I was in Petra's office with her, an RCMP officer, and two cops. I shouldn't have planned this meeting on the same day as seeing the rental agent. I was still in a fair bit of pain, and my stamina was more like *stami-not*. Victor had offered to come with me, but I'd sent him home. He looked much worse than I felt and shouldn't have been out in the first place.

The four officers sifted through the photocopies I'd brought along, and then they studied the files I'd copied onto a CD.

"Clever operation," Sergeant Mistry of the RCMP said.

"Yeah, these guys are good," the short Toronto cop said. "They must have put a lot of planning into this. I can't believe you stumbled onto their scheme."

"Stumbled isn't exactly the word for it," I said.

Petra jumped in. "We don't need to discuss how you came into possession of this information."

"Right," I said. "So what next?"

"This, on its own, isn't quite enough for probable cause," Mistry said. "We need some corroborating evidence."

"But if Rebecca has anything on her that she shouldn't when she comes back in through Canada Customs at the airport, then that's another story," Petra said.

I tuned out most of the rest of the conversation, since by now I was more or less peripheral. They planned to set up a multi-pronged sting, all of it contingent on what Rebecca had in her bags when she returned from the Bahamas on Monday.

"We'll need warrants for both galleries, and Darren's office and Ted's," insisted the taller Toronto cop, who hadn't said much until now.

"And surveillance on Christine, Ted, and Darren," the short city cop added.

"We can take Rebecca into custody at the airport if things unfold as we expect," Mistry said.

I left them to their plotting and went in search of Aspirin. I was halfway tempted to call Rebecca and borrow a few of her Percocets.

# *Tuesday, May 12, 12:53 p.m.*

"She had a forged Harris, Varley, Morrisseau, and two Chee Chees," I said.

"So would that be one Chee?" Lindsey asked.

"Very funny."

It was a sunny, gorgeous day, and Lindsey and I were having lunch at a sidewalk patio on College Street. We were far enough from the business core to not have to fight for a table with crowds of office drones determined to get some sun during their sixty-minute respite from their cubicle farms.

"The first two painters were in the Group of Seven, right?" Lindsey asked.

"Yes, and the other two are First Nations artists. Morrisseau is credited as the father of the Woodland school of art, and Chee Chee is in the generation that followed him."

"My, my, my, aren't we up on Canadian visual art history?"

"Not really. I looked it up on the Internet."

"What clued you in?"

"When I went to Christine's Harbourfront gallery, I saw a lot of stuff I remembered vaguely from a junior high school trip to Ottawa. We went to the National Art

Gallery. I suddenly remembered I'd seen a lot of those names in Darren's client files. That's when I first started to piece it together."

"But what made you think they were forged paintings made in the Bahamas?" Lindsey asked.

"I always had a funny feeling about Rebecca and her trips, even after she told me about Ephraim. I figured if she wasn't bringing cash or anything *in* to the Bahamas, then she must have been bringing something *out* of the Bahamas. I have no idea who made the paintings. She probably gave a description or a photo of what she wanted to some local starving artist and paid him cash to make a duplicate copy."

The waitress cleared our lunch plates and asked if we wanted dessert. Lindsey said she would look at the menu, but I wasn't interested. I still didn't have much appetite, so I just ordered lemonade.

"Unbelievable," Lindsey said. "So what about Ted? How'd he go from hottie to naughty?"

"It clicked when he told me he was in wine importing and exporting. I think I was so sensitive to things crossing borders that I flagged it. Then he mentioned importing that Pinot Grigio Rebecca threw in my face. It seemed too coincidental that it was her favourite wine. Meanwhile Ted said he rarely saw her. That was just too unlikely."

The midday sun was getting warmer, and I had no hat and no sunglasses. "Do you mind if we move to a table with an umbrella? I don't mind hanging out while you have dessert, but if I stay in the sun much longer, I'll get a headache."

"Sure, no problem."

Just as I was about to stand up, a pigeon shat on my head. "What the fuck? Oh, gross! Give me a tissue, serviette, something. *Yuck!*"

Lindsey reached for her purse, and as she did, she accidentally knocked over my glass of lemonade right onto my lap. I was wearing a light blue skirt, and the liquid made it almost transparent.

"Excuse me, miss," I said, "can you please bring the bill?"

After we paid our bill and headed out to Lindsey's car, she said before I could get in, "Here, sit on that newspaper. I don't want the seats to get sticky."

"Well, then, you shouldn't have dumped my drink on me."

We were soon driving east along Gerrard Street but kept hitting red lights.

"So how the hell did art forgery and everything in the Bahamas fit in with money laundering and insider trading?" Lindsey asked.

"I don't quite understand it myself. Basically, the four of them were playing both ends against the middle, through the middle, away from the middle. Christine sold the forged paintings Rebecca brought back from Freeport. Ted handled the logistics and freight-forwarding. He also helped find clients. People who buy private reserve wines and have their own cellars often like other finer things in life, too."

"Like art."

"Exactly. Christine would provide a fake provenance for the paintings, and Ted would help her arrange for private sales of the real ones. On the books she still seemed to have those paintings in her inventory. However, the paintings on display at the gallery are fakes. Most of them, anyway. I think she only processes a couple of forgeries a month."

"So Darren wasn't doing any insider trading, after all?"

"Actually, yes, he was. That's what was so confusing at first. The other side of the scam was that he'd wash the money by 'buying' a cheap painting from one of her galleries and 'selling' the same painting back to her other gallery for several thousand dollars."

"It was just a bloody revolving door of money. Unbelievable."

"I'm glad I cashed Ted's cheque before his accounts were frozen."

"So what's going to happen to them?"

"They're all on bail pending trial and they've all had their passports confiscated. Case closed."